THE **DELICIOUS DESIRES** SERIES

DELICIOUS
Complication

DELICIOUS
Complication

SABRINA SOL

Entangled Publishing, LLC
2614 South Timberline Road
Suite 105, PMB 159
Fort Collins, CO 80525
rights@entangledpublishing.com

Brazen is an imprint of Entangled Publishing, LLC.

Edited by Heather Howland
Cover design by LJ Anderson/Deposit Photos
Cover photography by VitalikRadko/Deposit Photos

Manufactured in the United States of America

First Edition September 2015

ENTANGLED
BRAZEN

To my auntie Elva
For kicking cervical cancer in the butt

Chapter One

What was it about weddings that made Daisy want to drink?

Okay, drink and cry.

And okay, sometimes the degree of crying was directly related to the degree of drinking.

But now that the happy tears were done for the day and her maid of honor/wedding planner duties were officially over, Daisy strolled through the hallways of the historic Hotel Esperanza in downtown Los Angeles determined to get her buzz on. The hotel's signature mix of old world architecture and modern decor had been the perfect setting for Amara's dream wedding. And it had meant everything to Daisy that she had helped give it to her.

Even the little voice in her head that usually criticized every move, every decision, had gone silent for once.

Daisy had done a great job, and she knew it.

She could still see the pure joy in her cousin's face as she walked down the aisle to meet Eric in front of the priest. Even Amara's parents, who had been against the idea of her dating him in the first place, couldn't stop smiling. It was a beautiful, traditional wedding. The exact opposite of what Daisy wanted. That is, *if* she ever decided to get married in the first place. Eloping to Vegas was more her style. No big wedding meant no hurt feelings when it came to the guest list. Especially when the bride would have to think long and hard about inviting her own mother.

None of that mattered right now anyway. She shook the troubling thoughts out of her head and went back to remembering that she'd just successfully pulled off her first official wedding planner job. She was still smiling when she finally reached the hotel's lounge area, but she stopped short of walking through the door. The source of her momentary hesitation—and new frown—sat at one end of the bar studying his empty shot glass as if debating whether he should fill it up again.

Of course. Brandon Montoya *would* be the one to ruin her plan to decompress alone. He had a special knack for annoying her whether he meant to or not. And usually he meant to.

How could she relax now that she'd have to be on her guard?

Especially when he looked like *that.*

She'd seen him in suits before—he wore them so often, they were like a second skin. But this one was different. The dark gray designer ensemble covering his black shirt fit his tall and muscular frame perfectly and dangerously. Combined with his gentleman's buzz cut and expertly groomed stubble, Brandon had walked into the church that day looking like he'd come straight from a *GQ* magazine cover photo shoot.

She'd tripped boobs-first into an altar boy at the sight.

He exuded sex, money, and ego. A triple threat that could cost any woman her panties with just a snap of his fingers.

And for the past several months, Daisy had been trying hard to hold onto hers.

Brandon was more than man candy. He was a savvy businessman and an important associate for both her and Amara. So it didn't help that bumblebees, instead of butterflies, attacked her insides whenever they were in the same room. Her attempts to hide her nervousness usually came off as outright bitchiness, and that made their encounters much more tense and exhausting than they needed to be.

And now Brandon was the only thing standing between Daisy and a well-deserved hangover.

She could always turn around and raid the minibar in the honeymoon suite instead. She'd reserved it for the newlyweds before Eric had surprised Amara with a trip to Hawaii and had forgotten to cancel. It was the excuse she'd needed to get good and drunk tonight. But did she really want to blow all her money on stale pretzels and Smurf-sized bottles of vodka?

She took a deep breath, squared her shoulders, and walked over to Brandon. "So, are you drowning your sorrows now that my cousin is off the market?"

She'd wanted it to sound like a joke. It didn't.

He glanced at her over his shoulder. She expected him to come back with some sort of biting comment, as per their usual banter. Instead, his full lips turned up into a lazy smile as his eyes traveled up and down her body, leaving behind a trail of goose bumps on her skin. "I have more than half a bottle left of this hotel's most expensive tequila. How can I be sad about anything?"

After months of watching Brandon flirt with her cousin, she expected him to be at least a little bummed, no matter how many times he denied the attraction. Maybe not. She shrugged. "Good point. I, on the other hand, am going to be drinking the hotel's *cheapest* tequila, and I'm pretty sure I won't be sad either after a couple of shots."

She kicked her shoes off, laid her purse on the counter, and sat on the stool next to him. She ignored the familiar pandemonium in her stomach when he reached over and pulled her stool closer. Cedar, musk, and other spices invaded her nostrils and she tried not to sigh in response. God, he smelled as delicious as he looked.

Brandon leaned close and whispered in her ear, "I'm willing to share if you're willing to behave yourself."

Despite his words, the way he breathed them against her skin made it sound like "behave" was the last thing he wanted her to do. She shook off the tingles traveling south from where his breath had warmed her neck, and that little voice in her head demanded she keep her game face on. Brandon was an OCC—an obsessive compulsive charmer. He flirted with anything in a skirt, or in her case, evening gown. And as part owner of one of the hottest restaurants in Los Angeles, he was also something of a celebrity. Which meant he was used to wooing glamorous models and actresses. It didn't matter that Daisy was neither of those things. He probably couldn't turn it off if he tried.

So she smiled and tipped her head to the side. "I'm always well behaved when it comes to you, Brandon. Hmm, maybe that's why I frustrate you so much?"

He opened his mouth to say something but then closed it. He turned away from her to motion for the bartender to bring over another shot glass. "You're lucky I don't feel like drinking alone tonight."

Was that a twinge of sadness in his voice? Instead of dishing out a flippant retort, she kept quiet while Brandon filled up both glasses. Then he handed her one. A quick whiff told her it was going to be strong. He knocked his own glass against hers. "*Salud.*"

"*Salud,*" she said and gulped the clear liquid down. The tequila immediately warmed her from the inside out. But it didn't burn her throat or make her wince. It went down smooth. No wonder the gold label stuff was so expensive. It tasted nothing like the paint-thinner crap she usually bought at the grocery store with her margarita mix.

"It's good, *verdad*?" Brandon didn't wait for her to answer and poured them both another round.

This time Daisy didn't wait for a toast. She threw her head back and, like a magician, made the drink disappear. When she saw Brandon's questioning expression, she shrugged again. "What? It's been a long day."

"I'm not judging. Believe me." And with that he downed his shot as well.

Daisy sighed as the stress slid off her body. "Tequila makes everything better."

Brandon laughed and nodded. "Everything except the next morning."

"True. But for tonight, it's exactly what I need."

"You and me both."

What the…? She twisted in her seat to look at him. "Oh my God. Are we actually agreeing on something?"

He grinned. "I think we are. See, I'm not so terrible."

"I never said you were terrible."

"Then why do our conversations always end in arguments?"

"They do not."

"Yes they do."

"They do… Ugh." She nudged her glass in his direction. "Can we just do another shot please?"

He chuckled. "Fine. I'll share more of my expensive tequila, but you have to tell me what's making you drink like this."

"How do you know I don't drink like this every night?" He raised his eyebrow, and she couldn't help but laugh. "What can I say? I guess I'm just relieved that everything went so well despite a few hiccups."

"What sort of hiccups? From what I could tell, everything

was perfect. You should be very proud of yourself, Daisy. You gave Amara and Eric a beautiful wedding."

The compliment caught her off guard. "Thank you. Well, I guess most everything was perfect. There were just little things here and there that only I would notice. And it didn't help that my ex-boyfriend showed up as the plus one of a second cousin I've hated since high school. Or that I found out tonight that they're engaged."

"Ouch," he said with a wince.

"Yep. And what sucks is that I shouldn't even care. I haven't seen Luis in over a *year* and I've dated my fair share of guys since then. So why the hell did I feel like kicking him in the groin when he told me? And why am I even telling you—of all people—this."

"It's the tequila."

She sighed and held up her glass. "It is. Now pour me another shot."

"Are you sure you can handle a third one?"

"I can if you can."

This time he turned sideways to look at her. "Did you just question my man card?"

Daisy snorted. "Your man card? Did you just use those words? Dear lord, you're drunker than I thought. I should cut you off."

"First of all, I'm not drunk. Not even close. And B, I've had the fucking day from hell, so if I want to chug this entire goddamn bottle, no one is going to stop me."

She raised her hands like a Western movie outlaw. "Whoa there, Mr. Sensitive. I was just joking about the tequila." Daisy reached down and slowly pushed the bottle closer to him. He nodded and studied his glass again. She'd never seen Brandon brood before. As much as she hated to do it, she finally asked, "Do you want to talk about it?" He looked at her like she had three heads. "I mean I'm definitely not an expert when it comes to relationships but obviously I know a lot about rejection so—"

"What are you saying?"

"I'm saying I get it. You're pissed that Amara married Eric."

He dragged his hand over his face. "Amara has nothing to do with why I'm drinking. I'm happy for her and for Eric. She's a friend and a business partner. That's all. I don't know how many more times I can explain that to you."

"If this isn't about Amara, then who? What woman could possible drive the great playboy restaurateur Brandon Montoya to drink?"

"My mother. I found out today that she has cancer." He shook his head and refilled their glasses.

Shit. Way to drag everyone down, Daisy.

Without worrying what he might think for once, she reached out and touched his arm. "I'm sorry. Is there anything I can do?"

"I doubt it. Alex and I are flying home to Puerto Rico tomorrow so we can talk to her doctors."

Daisy nodded. Alex was actually Alexa, Brandon's twin sister. He'd always wanted a brother, so the nickname stuck. Despite his constant teasing, they had a very close relationship and, in fact, she was co-owner and executive chef of his L.A. Cuchara restaurant. It was good that they were both going to Puerto Rico. Hopefully, once they knew exactly what their mom was facing, it would help Brandon feel like he had some control over the situation. She'd known him less than year, but it was obvious that he was a man who hated to not be the one calling the shots.

The mood had darkened drastically. A depressed Brandon was worse than a smart-ass Brandon. Time for some small talk about things non-cancer related.

"So, how long has it been since you've gone back to

Puerto Rico?"

He traced the rim of his still full glass with a finger. "Just over two years. I visited right before I moved here from New York."

"Do you miss it?"

"Sure. Besides my mom, I have other family there. And, of course, I miss the food."

"Really? Seems to me that Alexa could probably cook you up anything you wanted."

"Yes, but there's something to be said about eating food in the place where it originated. I've been all over the world and there's nothing like having Coq Au Vin in France or Pizza Margarita in Italy or even beignets in New Orleans. And, for me, Puerto Rico is my *mamá's asopao*."

"What is that? Soup?"

"It's more like a gumbo or even a paella. She makes hers with chicken and *chorizo*, ham and rice. And the broth is this hearty, succulent juice seasoned with oregano and *chile* peppers, tomatoes and garlic. My sister may be a James Beard Award nominee, but even she can't make an *asopao* like my *mamá*."

Her mouth watered. "Sounds delicious."

"It is. If you ever go to Puerto Rico, you should try some."

"Guess I'll just have to take your word for it. No way am I ever going to Puerto Rico."

"Why?" he asked and turned toward her, leaning his elbow on the bar. "What's wrong with Puerto Rico?"

"Nothing. Except that you can only get there by air or cruise ship."

"And?"

"And every other month there's some news story about a horrible disease breaking out on a cruise ship. Experiencing dysentery with hundreds of other people and no working bathrooms is not my idea of a vacation. So no cruises for me.

Ever."

"Then take a plane. You know flying is the safest way to travel."

"Why do people always say that? Do you own stock in an airline or something?"

"No, but it's true. I fly all the time."

"*You* have to fly because of your business. *I* don't have to fly anywhere. And I plan on keeping it that way."

He hooted with laughter. "Daisy Robles, are you telling me that you're afraid of flying?"

She knocked back the third shot and shook her head. "Nope. I'm not afraid of flying. I'm afraid of *crashing*."

Brandon laughed even harder. So hard that she could see tears in his eyes. As much as she liked seeing his mood lift, she hated to be the source of his amusement. Familiar pricks of annoyance stabbed at the back of her neck. "I don't see what's so funny."

"It's just…you try to act like you're this tough, independent woman, and it turns out you're not so tough after all. It's… satisfying."

Her irritation shot to threat level orange. "Whatever. You're not perfect either."

"I never said I was."

Daisy slapped a hand on the bar. "Are you kidding me? Your whole life is about projecting perfection. Your hair, this suit, your car…the women you date. I'd be careful if I were you, Brandon. If you date any more Barbies, the tabloids are going to start calling you Ken. And we all know what poor Ken was missing."

She lowered her eyes to his crotch and Brandon followed them. Then his head snapped back up and his laser stare went straight to her lips. "Trust me. The Barbies have no complaints. But if you don't believe me, I'm happy to prove it to you, since I know you've been wondering."

Invisible flames rushed up her face, burning her with both embarrassment and lust. She knew it had been a bad idea to drink with Brandon. She'd become too loose, too comfortable. And—before they started talking about his mom—she had started to become a little turned on. Damn alcohol.

Still, there was no way in hell she would ever admit he'd come close to the truth. He'd make fun of her again. Or worse, he'd sleep with her and then in the morning do whatever he could to make the situation go away.

Daisy had been tossed aside by enough people in her life. She wasn't about to add a celebrity restaurant owner to the list. "Sorry, buddy. But there's not enough tequila in this world."

She watched his jaw muscle tense and knew she hit a nerve. Then his expression relaxed. "Suit yourself," he said with a shrug before finally downing his shot. "Anyway, we both know you're not my type. I like my women a little less bossy."

Angry, mortified, and tipsy, Daisy jumped off the stool and bent to pick up her shoes. She tried to think of one last snarky comeback to toss at him before storming out of the bar. But when she stood back up, she couldn't even form the words. It wasn't her temper that left her speechless—it was the sight, just beyond Brandon's shoulder, of her ex and that *bruja* Ginger snuggling in a corner booth.

Brandon noticed her still standing there and waved his hand. "Hello? I thought you were leaving?"

Daisy dropped her shoes and quickly slid her stool out of the way so she could reach to pull his hand down. That's when Luis caught her eye and waved. "Great. Just great," she muttered. "Now he knows I'm here."

"Who knows?" Brandon moved as if to turn his head to see who Daisy was staring at.

"No. Don't look."

But it was too late. Brandon looked and then Luis awkwardly waved at him, too. He whispered something in Ginger's ear, and she nodded. Daisy watched as her ex called the waitress over. Her stomach sank. They were going to come over for a chat. She knew it. It had been awful enough to have to fake a smile every time she ran into them during the reception. But now, with a few tequila shots in her, Daisy doubted she could playact one more time. She was fired up from the last rumble with Brandon, in more ways than one. There was no telling what she'd do if that witch waved her gaudy ring in front of her again. It would be bad for her to make a scene, or worse, get thrown out for making a scene. How could she hope to plan another wedding at the hotel if the owners had a restraining order against her?

She needed a buffer. Something or someone to make sure that she didn't make a complete ass of herself.

That's when the most ridiculous idea popped into Daisy's head. So ridiculous she had to cover her mouth to stifle the giggle threatening to erupt. The man *was* dealing with the news that his mom had cancer. He'd probably never go for it. But as she watched Luis pay his tab, her ridiculous idea started sounding better and better.

"Kiss me," she blurted to Brandon as Luis and Ginger stood up from their table.

Brandon choked on the drink he'd just taken. "Excuse me?"

"Look, I hate being *that* girl but, screw it, I am. So kiss me."

"You just said there wasn't enough tequila in the world."

"Yeah, well. Desperate times call for desperate measures. Kiss my lips. Now."

"Desperate? Forget it. You're crazy if you think I'm going to kiss you after you just insulted me."

"Oh my God. Would you do something useful with that

tongue of yours for once and kiss—"

Brandon pulled her toward him and kissed her—hard—and his mouth swallowed up the rest of her sentence. At first, she was too shocked to kiss him back. Her eyes had been focused on Luis and Ginger walking toward them. But as Brandon's warm tongue pressed forward, seeking entry, she no longer saw anything or anyone. She opened to him and he released a low groan that weakened her knees. She wrapped her arms around his neck, and he pulled her further into his chest. Her heart thumped madly as the rest of her body hummed with desire.

Holy hell. She wanted Brandon. Bad.

The sound of someone clearing his throat jerked her back into consciousness, and she pulled her tongue out of Brandon's mouth. Their eyes met briefly, and the desire reflected in his gaze sent another blast of heat through her. She turned away so as to not melt into his arms one more time and faced an uncomfortable-looking Luis and an open-mouthed Ginger.

"Oh, hey guys. Are you heading home now?" She tried to sound nonchalant despite the fact Brandon had pulled her backward until she stood between his legs and hooked one of his arms around her waist.

"Yeah. We decided to have one last nightcap," Luis said. He smiled at her but his eyes fell on Brandon.

The two couples stood there in silence for a few seconds before Luis reached out his hand to Brandon. "I don't think we've met. I'm Luis Arroyo and this is my fiancée Ginger Soto."

Brandon uncurled his arm from Daisy and shook Luis's hand. "Good to meet you. I'm Brandon Montoya, Daisy's boyfriend."

Chapter Two

Ginger's mouth opened again.

"Brandon Montoya? As in the owner of the L.A. Cuchara restaurant in downtown?"

His head was still processing the fact that he'd kissed Daisy—and that it was even more spectacular than he'd ever imagined. So he was a little slow in responding to Ginger. Then Daisy answered for him. "Yes. *That* Brandon Montoya." And although he couldn't see her face, he heard her smile.

Luis shook Brandon's hand a second time. "Oh. Wow. It's good to meet you, too. I had no idea Daisy was dating a celebrity. I hear the food in your restaurant is fantastic. Maybe one day we'll be lucky enough to get a reservation. Last time I tried, there was a two-month waiting list."

Now he was the one smiling. He loved hearing that his restaurant was on someone's hot list—even if it was some squirrely-looking guy who, for some reason, was making Daisy act very un-Daisy like. It wasn't any of his business who she wanted to make jealous. With that one shocking kiss, he'd signed up for the ride. Might as well play along. "Well any friend of Daisy's is a friend of mine. Just let her know the next time you want to come in, and I'll make sure you get on the list." Brandon practically gasped out the last part of the sentence thanks to Daisy's elbow jab into his stomach.

"Thanks, man. Daisy, I think I still have your number so I'll text you later this week and let you know."

"Sure, Luis. You do that," she said after elbowing Brandon again. He liked it better when it was just the two of them pretending to be hot for each other.

Although, that kiss felt pretty real.

"Well, it's getting late. We should get going. Right, babe?" The way Ginger smiled at Luis, he knew the poor guy would not be texting Daisy this week…or ever.

"Nice to see you both. Thanks again for coming," Daisy said.

They stood in silence as they watched Luis and Ginger walk out of the bar. Then Daisy turned around and socked Brandon smack dab in the shoulder.

"Ouch! What was that for? You already jabbed me for the comment about him coming to restaurant. Twice." What the hell? Hadn't he just saved the day?

"You're right. Those were for giving him an excuse to call me. But the punch was for kissing me…like that."

"You asked me to. What was I supposed to do? Give you a peck on the cheek? I figured kissing you thoroughly was the best way to convince them we were a couple. Plus I don't remember you complaining all that much during."

There was no way she could deny just how much she'd enjoyed it. No way he could either.

Based on her shocked expression, he braced himself for another assault. But she didn't hit or slap him. Instead, she blew her hair out of her face and sat back down on the stool next to him. "Sorry. How about you return the favor and hit me back…with another shot?" She pushed her empty glass in his direction. "And thanks for doing that—you know, the whole pretending to be my boyfriend thing. You're having a bad day and didn't have to play along, but you did and I appreciate it. I owe you one."

Part of him wanted to ask if he could take another kiss as repayment. It surprised him just how much he still savored the first one. Not just because it was so hot, but because for those few seconds against her lips, all worry about his *mamá* was pushed to the back of his mind. He'd become lost in the taste and feel of her, and he desperately needed to get lost all over again. That was why he hadn't gone home right away after the reception. Brandon had walked into that hotel bar looking for some sort of remedy for his pain, something to help him forget about what he'd have to deal with tomorrow and in the coming weeks. The tequila mixed with some Daisy could be the potent antidote he was looking for.

He reached for the bottle of tequila but she grabbed it before he could and examined the label. "Damn. This must've cost you a pretty penny."

He shrugged. "Some things in life are worth it."

"Sure. Things like food and a house or a car. Only a rich person could justify spending a small fortune on a bottle of alcohol that, based on the amount of shots we've done so far, isn't even going to last one night."

"Why must you always over-analyze things?"

He saw her bristle at his accusation. "I'm not. All I'm saying is that money can't buy you happiness."

"Sure it can. Money bought me this bottle of tequila which is making me very happy."

She studied him for a second before shaking her head. "You're hopeless, you know that?"

"And you're killing my buzz. God, Daisy, for once in your life can you *not* worry about how much something costs or why someone is offering it to you? Can't you just drink and enjoy?"

Man, she was getting under his skin tonight. In more ways than one. He could blame the tequila and the rotten news he'd received. Although the truth was, the woman knew how to push his buttons. When she wasn't making him crazy hot, she was making him crazy. Especially when she criticized his lifestyle. He worked his ass off to get the things he had. So what if he liked to indulge now and then? Who was she to judge him?

He expected her to either argue with him again or get up and leave. So he was surprised when she did neither.

"Fine," she said with a sigh. "I'll sit here and enjoy your expensive tequila. Although I think it would be ten times better with some salt and limes."

"*Aye* Daisy, this isn't some race where the goal is to drink as much as you can as fast as you can. No, you need to take your time with this tequila. It deserves to be savored and tasted thoroughly."

As if she wanted to taste it again, she licked her lips. The memory of those lips against his made him shift in his seat. Brandon snuck another look at the way her tanned cleavage strained against the fabric of her pale-colored dress and the way wisps of her dark hair framed her smooth neck.

He couldn't deny the very *hard* effect she was having on his body. He wanted her. Correction. He needed her. Because anything that made him forget about his trip to Puerto Rico the next day—even if only for a few hours—was a welcomed distraction. He needed Daisy Robles naked and underneath him as soon as possible.

Easier said than done, of course. He'd already pissed her off once tonight. If he had any chance of convincing her that she, too, wanted to be naked and underneath him, then he had to play nice.

Nice now. Naughty later.

Brandon smiled and raised his hand to signal the bartender, never once breaking the intense gaze between them. "On second thought, we'll try it your way. But let's take this party of two out to the veranda. The night is still young, and I've been itching to smoke the cigar I just bought."

To his surprise, she didn't protest. He let the bartender know where they were moving and what they needed. Then he followed a barefoot Daisy outside.

He motioned for her to take a seat at one of the small patio tables. He took the seat next to her and set down their bottle of tequila in front of him. Within minutes, the bartender appeared and set out new shot glasses, a saltshaker, and a small plate of lime wedges.

After the waiter left, Brandon filled their glasses. "Ladies first," he said with a wink.

Maybe it was the crisp night air, or the fact it had been a very long day for her, but Daisy didn't hesitate. She licked the inside of her left wrist, salted it, chugged down the very expensive tequila like it was an oyster shooter, licked her wrist again and then sucked hard on a lime wedge. "God, that's good stuff. It's definitely better this way," she whispered and closed her eyes.

He grew harder after the quick glimpse of her tongue on her own skin. If anyone had told him a few hours ago that he was going to try and seduce Daisy tonight, he would've tossed good money their way and told them to go try their luck somewhere else. But after all the shots they'd already done and that fucking kiss, Brandon was ready to do exactly that. He ached for her now and couldn't think of anything else.

The antidote was working.

Brandon reached out and grabbed her wrist. Her eyes flew open. "What are you doing?"

"Since you insisted the tequila was better after licking the salt off your wrist, I figured I'd try it the same way."

"I…um…that's not what I meant."

"Maybe you should be clearer next time."

"Maybe you should listen better."

He shrugged but didn't release her wrist. "I'm listening now."

The air crackled between them. A warning perhaps that whatever happened next would change things, complicate things. She must have sensed it, too. Her face flushed in the moonlight, and she bit her bottom lip.

The woman was sexy as hell.

"What are we doing?" she whispered.

"We're doing shots."

"Again, that's not what I meant."

"Fine. We're just two friends and business associates enjoying some fine tequila and getting to know each other better." He tried to sound matter-of-fact, but the wild look in her eyes was making it difficult.

"Oh, so that's what this is? You just want to get to know me better?"

"Yes. We'll sit here for a while, drink, and learn some new things about each other. We can even make a game out of it. We each have to tell something about ourselves before we do the shot. If the other person already knows it, then you have to do a second one."

Brandon had played games involving alcohol before. But none had excited him more than the thought of playing this one against Daisy. He could almost see the argument going on in her head. Knowing her, she was debating all of the risks.

After a few seconds, she finally sighed in resignation. "Fine, I'll play. But I have to warn you, I may be little but I can hold my liquor pretty well. So don't be disappointed when I don't drop any deep, dark secrets."

He tried not to smirk. "We'll see about that. Just to be on the safe side, perhaps you better give me your car keys."

"Not necessary. I'm staying overnight at the hotel. Why don't you give me yours?"

"Not necessary. I took a cab over here and I can take a cab home. Guess that settles things. Let's start the game. I'll go first."

She inhaled as he turned her palm over and sprinkled salt onto the inside of her wrist. And just before he took a lick, he stared into her eyes and said, "I think you are one hell of a sexy woman, Daisy Robles."

• • •

Daisy's insides clenched as soon as Brandon's warm, wet tongue slid along her skin. He finished his drink and the lime wedge all while staring at her. He was the one who took the shot but it felt as if she had. Warmth spread across her chest, up her neck, and across her cheeks. Her limbs loosened, her breathing deepened. She'd become drunk on his words. On him.

She needed to sober up. Quick. He was playing a game with her and it had nothing to do with alcohol. She needed her wits about her if she was going to stand a chance of beating him at his own game.

"You think you're being so smooth trying to sneak in a comment like that. Besides, you're not even following your own rules. That wasn't about you, it was about me. So I think you need to take another shot."

He leaned in closer to her, obviously enjoying her reaction. "I disagree. Unless, of course, you already knew that I thought that about you? Tell me, Daisy. Did you know that I think you're so fucking sexy that I can't think straight sitting this close to you?"

His bluntness shocked her, yet also undeniably turned her on. He was baiting her to move their conversation into dangerous territory. She decided to move it back on solid ground.

"Fine. My turn." She grabbed everything from him and readied her shot. "Did you know I think you can be pretty arrogant sometimes?" Before she could see his reaction she licked the salt from her wrist, squeezed her eyes shut, and drank. When she opened them, Brandon was pouring her another shot.

"Sorry, but I already knew that. Take a second shot."

"No you didn't."

"Sure I did. I knew it from day one. You're not exactly subtle with your facial expressions or words. I bet you're a lousy poker player."

It was true. Ever since Amara had partnered with Brandon's restaurant, Daisy couldn't help thinking he had some ulterior motive for helping her business. But he'd been nothing but professional and respectful—even toward her—and he'd never called her out on her attitude toward him. She grew defensive. "It's because I didn't trust you. I was only protecting my cousin."

"I know," he said with a shrug. "Now drink."

She complied only because she wasn't sure what else to say. Guilt seeped through her alcohol buzz. Brandon had not only helped save Amara's bakery, he was responsible for helping her launch her own event planning business. His restaurant was one of the hottest spots in L.A. right now and she'd been able to secure some pretty nice jobs thanks to him and his customers. Although her mind told her she should feel bad, the tequila now flowing through her veins only made her feel good. Too good.

"I think I may have hit my limit. I need some air."

"Daisy, we're already outside."

"Oh, yeah, we are. Well, I think I need some air from over there." She pointed to the balcony's railing. Praying that her legs weren't completely filled with jelly, she stood up and stalked to the edge of the patio's balcony. A passing breeze cooled her instantly, and her head cleared. She wasn't drunk. Yet. After taking a few deep breaths, she felt like herself again. But then Brandon approached her from behind and the wooziness returned. She tried to focus on the amazing view before her instead of on him.

"The city looks beautiful from up here, doesn't it?" he said. "Funny how the things that you see every day can suddenly look so different once you change your point of view."

"It's breathtaking," she agreed.

"Breathtaking is exactly the word I was thinking." His low, odd tone made her turn around…and inhale sharply. He was looking at her, rather than the cityscape down below them. The look in his eyes sent those familiar shivers through her body again, and this time they went straight to her nipples, making them pebble underneath her strapless bra.

"You're cold. Here, take my jacket." He undid one button and opened it. She fought the urge to wrap her arms around his chest so he could warm her up with his body instead. But she knew that touching him wouldn't just warm her, it would ignite her. So she stayed put.

"I'm fine."

"Just take it." She inhaled as he held it out in front of her. She turned her back to him and slid her arms into the oversized sleeves. But the breath she'd been holding for those few seconds came out in a rush once his hands stilled on her shoulders.

"So I just thought of another thing you probably don't know about me," he said.

"What's that?"

"It's taking every ounce of will power I have to not think about that kiss and how you tasted. *Todavía te pruebo en mis labios*."

She touched her lips. She could still taste him, too. Her heart pounded and her mind jumbled. Was this another one of his silly games? And why on earth did she want to play, despite knowing any night spent with Brandon would be one night only?

The memory of that searing kiss came rushing back, kicking her pulse up by a thousand notches. What he said earlier was true. She had enjoyed it. And now she craved it. So much so that she knew she wouldn't be right until she experienced it again.

She turned slowly to face him. His arms fell away, and she instantly missed his touch.

Just one more time, she promised herself. One more kiss and she'd say good night and show him that she could flirt and tempt as much as he could without it having to mean a thing.

She grabbed his head between her hands and brought his lips down to hers, smugly enjoying his surprised expression before closing her eyes and losing herself in his warm mouth.

He let her control the tempo at first, their tongues languidly reacquainting themselves, their hands roaming each other's bodies in timid exploration. But the build-up of passion eventually exploded, and their movements turned from composed to urgent as Brandon backed her up against the railing. He moved his lips to her neck. "*Maldicion!* Why in the hell didn't we do this sooner?" he rasped.

She knew exactly why. Because he terrified her. Or rather she was terrified of the way he made her feel. For as much as she sometimes wanted to strangle him, she also wanted to screw him. Afraid she'd tell him as much, she put her hands on his head again and brought him back to her lips. His hands moved from her waist to her breasts and she sighed in pleasure. A subtle vibration startled her and for a second she was impressed with his skills. But when the vibration persisted, she realized it was coming from the pocket of his jacket and not from between her legs.

"I think your phone is buzzing," she murmured between kisses. When he didn't answer, she broke away from his grasp and pulled out the phone. Her words must've finally registered, and Brandon took a step back as he reached for it. It buzzed one last time in her hand and she looked down at the screen.

"Sorry about that. I'll turn it off," Brandon said as he swiped his fingers across the phone.

"If you need to make a call, I don't mind." It would give her a chance to catch her breath and clear her head.

Brandon shoved the phone into his pants pocket. "It's fine. I'm sure he'll leave a message if it's important."

"I didn't know you knew Christian Santos. That was him, right? The *telenovela* actor?"

He pulled her into an embrace. "He's one of my best customers and has become a good friend, too." Brandon lowered his head for another kiss. She kissed him back, her mouth open and accepting of it all. Eventually he moved his lips to her neck again, and she took the opportunity to speak while her mouth was free.

"He's getting married, right? I read in *People* magazine that she's not even an actress or a model. Just a regular girl he met in Whole Foods."

Brandon continued with his warm nibbles and licks. "Well, if it's in *People* magazine then I guess it must be true," he whispered between kisses on her collarbone. "I didn't realize you were a celebrity groupie."

"I'm not a groupie. I just think it's interesting that you're friends with Christian Santos, that's all." She sighed as he focused on consuming one of her earlobes. "So, how good of friends are you?"

This time he raised his head to look at her. "What do you mean? Have we smoked cigars and drunk brandy together?

Sure. Lots of times. Is he going to ask me to be his best man? I doubt it. Why?"

"Well, I was thinking that maybe next time he comes into the restaurant you could call me and I could come by. I'd love a chance to meet him and his fiancée. Who knows? Maybe I could even convince them to let me be their wedding planner."

"Are you serious?"

The slight chuckle after his words straightened her back. "Of course I am. Do you know what planning a wedding like that would mean for my business?"

"I don't know, Daisy. He's a very important customer, and I don't know if I feel right pushing you on him like that."

"Why not? You give me referrals all the time."

It was true. When Daisy had announced earlier in the year that she wanted to start her own event planning business, he'd offered to give her a couple of referrals to get the ball rolling. So far she'd done his accountant's fiftieth wedding anniversary and a graduation barbecue for a news anchor's son. But a Hollywood wedding? That was on a whole other level. An event like that could get people—important people—talking about her business. Then she wouldn't have to rely on Brandon or Amara to pass on jobs.

Brandon rubbed the back of his neck. "I don't know…"

"You don't think I'm good enough." The realization made her step away from him.

"I don't think you have enough experience. You just started this business. Besides Amara's wedding, how many other weddings have you done?"

"None."

"Exactly. And while this was a very nice wedding, I highly doubt it cost more than, what, ten thousand?" He took her silence as confirmation and continued. "I didn't think so. And knowing how much Christian is willing to spend on a bottle of wine, you can bet his wedding will be expensive."

"And what? You're afraid if it goes bad, that I'll embarrass you?"

"I didn't say that."

"You didn't have to. It's all over your face. Who's the bad poker player now?" She slid out of his jacket and pushed it against his chest.

He reached for her. "Daisy...I didn't mean to hurt your feelings. Can't we forget about this and go back to learning new things about each other?"

She backed away before he could touch her. "And I just learned that all those celebrity gossip magazines are true. You are an ass." This time she walked away from him before he could see just how deep his words had cut her.

She grabbed her purse and stormed back into the bar, stopping only to pick up the pair of heels she'd left behind. She made it all the way to the lobby elevator before a hand grabbed her wrist and spun her around. She came face-to-face with Brandon. "What the hell are you doing?"

"We weren't done...talking," he said in a low voice. Why did his eyes tell her they weren't done doing other things as well?

"*I* was." She yanked herself out of his grasp and pushed the button for the elevator. She closed her eyes and willed her nerves—and arousal—to disappear. She blamed both on the shots.

"Didn't your *mamá* teach you it's not nice to walk away from people when they're trying to apologize to you...or kiss you?" Brandon growled from behind her.

"My *mamá* didn't raise me, my dad did, and he taught me how to inflict all sorts of pain on someone who won't leave me alone. So if you'd like to use certain body parts after tonight, I suggest you go call yourself a cab. Now. "

The elevator doors opened and an elderly couple walked

out. She escaped inside and pressed the button for the tenth floor repeatedly. Much to her chagrin, he followed her.

The doors closed and he stood directly in front of her. His eyes focused on her mouth and she bit her lip. The air became thick. She took a deep breath, afraid she'd suffocate from just the presence of him.

"So, we're back to you pretending that everything I say pisses you off? I guess that means you don't want to kiss anymore?"

"Yes."

"Yes, you do want me to kiss you again?"

"Yes. No. God, you're so infuriating."

"Damn. You're eyes turn dark brown when you're all hot and bothered. I wonder what color they turn when you're worked up in a different way?" She could still smell the tequila on his breath. Why did that excite her? He moved closer and she closed her eyes. "I don't think you're really mad at me. I think you're really mad at yourself because even though you want to hate me, you also want to be fucked. By *me*."

The doors opened. A group of rowdy college kids—based on their licensed sweatshirts and baseball caps—fell inside. Drunk, every last one of them. Brandon moved again. This time, he stepped behind her and pulled her with him against the back wall of the elevator.

"If you really don't want this, tell me and I'll get off on the next floor," he whispered against her ear. "We'll pretend none of this ever happened and go back to the way things were before you walked into the bar tonight. Tell me you don't want this. Say the words."

She stared at the floor numbers as they ticked away on the display screen above the elevator doors. Time was running out.

Tell him Daisy. Say it before things go to far.

The elevator lurched and she stumbled backward until

her ass grazed his upper thigh. The hard bulge in his pants jerked against her, and she knew at that moment she didn't want to fight this anymore. His arousal and need thrilled her, filled her with a sense of power she hadn't felt in a long time. Maybe she wasn't good enough to impress one of his famous friends, but she was sure as hell good enough to make him lose control. So what if it was only one night? She'd make sure it was one night he'd never forget.

This time, Daisy pushed herself further into him on purpose. Her breath hitched as his right arm reached around and his fingers slightly brushed the side of her breast before encircling her waist.

She clamped her lips tight before a sigh escaped. The doors opened again and the group of drunk college kids spilled out. The doors closed again but Daisy and Brandon didn't move.

By floor number seven, his lips were on her neck and she fell into him more, if that was even possible. He moved his hands to both of her breasts, cupping and caressing them through her dress. By floor number eight, her hands were on the side of his thighs, and she was purposefully grinding against his crotch.

Floor number nine. He'd had enough. With a grunt, he spun her around and found her mouth, open and waiting for his total consumption.

Floor number ten. He pulled her into the hallway, murmuring and asking her for her room number. She tried to gain perspective even as his thumbs rubbed her nipples into hardened peaks. Taking his hand, she led him down past four or five rooms but before she could reach for the keycard in her purse, he pushed her body with his against the door and captured her mouth in another all-consuming kiss.

The clattering of glasses and plates from just a few feet away pulled her away from total surrender. She opened up her eyes just in time to see a hotel employee pushing a cart out of a nearby room. The stark realization of what she was doing and *who* she was doing it with was as sobering and shocking as a slap across the face.

Madre de dios. Brandon Montoya's hand is on my ass.

She tried to relax as he gathered her dress behind her and slowly inched it up the back of her thigh.

Think sexy thoughts. Think sexy thoughts.

What was wrong with her? How could she not be automatically thinking sexy thoughts when one of the sexiest men she knew had his tongue in her mouth, one hand on her boob, and another one dangerously close to her three-day-old Brazilian?

As Brandon moved to nibble on her ear, Daisy noticed the hotel employee with the cart was now staring at them. "Someone's watching us," she whispered to Brandon.

"Let them enjoy the show," he whispered back and slid his hand underneath the layers of her gown.

The hotel employee looked away and directed his cart down the hallway toward the elevator. Even though they no longer had an audience, Daisy debated again as to whether she should stop things before they went any further.

Then he brushed his fingers against the edge of her thong.

Electricity pulsed throughout her body, turning her blood into lava and melting her insides. She willed him silently to push his finger past the flimsy material and into her sex. But he didn't move. He just stared at her, through her, with dark, wild eyes. His gaze was as hot as his touch.

Words weren't needed. She knew what he waiting for. It was the same thing she was waiting for. With one slight move of her hip, his finger grazed the smooth, delicate skin underneath her panties. His dark eyes widened before he captured her mouth in another devastating kiss. It had been months since the last time someone kissed her. But Brandon wasn't just kissing her, he was *destroying* her. And as his finger teased her clitoris with soft strokes, she ached for even further destruction.

"So am I going to fuck you right here in the hallway or are we going to go inside? And just so you know, I'm good to go either way."

She was about to reach for her keycard when through her half-closed eyes she thought she saw a flash of light. Maneuvering her body away from his, Daisy tried to regain her wits.

This time Brandon seemed to also be trying to focus on their surroundings. "What's wrong?" he asked and turned around.

"I thought I saw something."

They both looked, but the hallway was empty. She could swear someone had been watching them again.

Or maybe you're just looking for excuses to stop this before it's too late.

Brandon grabbed her hand, lifted it to his lips, and kissed it. "What's going on, Daisy? You can tell me if you're having second thoughts about…this."

As soon as he said the words, she knew she couldn't go through with it. The fog lifted. Her mind cleared. As desperately as she wanted to feel Brandon inside her, it wasn't enough for her to forget who he was—an OCC looking for a one-night stand only. Sleeping with her was merely a means to scratch an itch or forget about his crappy day. Everything he'd said to her, everything he'd done, was nothing more than an attempt to get her into bed. He would've said those things to any woman tonight. She just happened to be the one who had sat down next to him at the bar.

Sleeping with him while knowing all of this would definitely hurt their professional relationship, because she'd never forgive herself for being such a dope. That wouldn't be good for her business or Amara's bakery. She couldn't go through with it no matter how good it had felt.

Daisy looked at the floor, embarrassment flaming her cheeks even more so than before. "I'm sorry."

"Stop. You don't have to apologize. I get it. Sleeping together would complicate things, and neither of us likes complications, do we?"

"I hope you don't think I meant for this to happen."

"Same here."

"Then can we just forget this and go back to being…"

"Friends?"

"I was going to say business associates. But, I guess we're more than that now."

"I guess so."

She reached out her hand. "Friends?"

He took it. "Friends," he said. Although he smiled, she noticed he barely gripped her hand.

"Look, you're still welcome to spend the night. It's late and the suite has a pull-out couch."

"It's okay. I'll just go down to the lobby and book my own room."

"The hotel is sold out this weekend. There are no rooms. Come inside and get some sleep."

"It's fine. Really. I'll call a cab."

"Would you stop? I'm trying to be a grown-up here. We can spend the night in the same room without it leading to something else. Friends, remember?"

Brandon agreed and after several uncomfortable minutes, he was settled on the couch and she was lying by herself on the king-size bed replaying the events of the day. Although she tried to focus on the happy things that had happened during the wedding and reception, thoughts of Brandon kissing her and touching her made her toss and turn.

In fact, sleep didn't come to her until almost three-thirty

in the morning, when she heard Brandon leave the room.

She already knew she'd wake up with a headache. If anyone asked, she'd blame her bloodshot eyes and crabby mood on the drinking.

Because no way was anyone ever going to find out that she almost slept with Brandon Montoya.

Chapter Three

Brandon had been back in Los Angeles for less than twenty-four hours and he'd already reached his frustration limit when it came to traffic gridlock. Thanks to construction detours and roadside fender benders, it had taken him almost an hour to travel a mere fifteen miles from his condo in Los Feliz to his lawyer's office in downtown.

When he finally entered the first floor lobby of the twenty-story high rise that was home to the office of Tucker, Miller, Perez & Associates, Brandon was officially ten minutes late for his nine o'clock appointment. He stepped inside the elevator and pressed the button for the eighteenth floor.

Thankfully he was all alone. He leaned sideways against the elevator wall and closed his eyes. Although he'd hoped to use the next several seconds to calm down his worked up nerves, flashes of the last time he'd been in an elevator invaded his mind and worked up another part of his body. It had only been two weeks since he'd almost slept with Daisy, yet it seemed like another lifetime ago.

The elevators doors opened, saving him from having to

relive it in his head for the umpteenth time.

"Good morning, Mr. Montoya. It's so nice to see you as always," the redhead at the reception desk purred when he walked up to her.

"It's nice to see you, too. Is he ready for me?" For the life of him, he couldn't remember the redhead's name. Usually he enjoyed flirting with her, but today he just wasn't in the mood. Maybe it was the traffic. Maybe it was everything that had happened in Puerto Rico the past two weeks.

Or maybe it's because she's not Daisy.

The thought seemed ridiculous. Why would he even think it?

"Look at who they let back into town." The booming voice of his lawyer and good friend Dante Perez interrupted his thoughts. Brandon nodded to the redhead and walked over to Dante, who was standing just beyond the lobby. His friend reached out and shook his hand. "How have you been, *compadre*?"

"I was fine until I had to drive on the freeway. Made me miss Puerto Rico."

"I bet. And Lorena? How is she?"

"Stubborn as always."

"Well, she *is* your mother."

"That's what she likes to tell me. Oh, and she sends her love and wants to know when you're going to go visit her because she knows a girl."

They exchanged knowing looks and his friend smiled and shook his head. His mother had given up a long time ago on setting Brandon up with the nice Catholic girls she met at her church. However, she was determined to still play matchmaker for Dante, who she insisted must be a long lost son of her favorite singer Julio Iglesias because of his dark hair, dark eyes, and year-round natural tan. Brandon always insisted his friend had no problem finding girlfriends on his own. But that didn't deter his mother. "I'm not going to find him a girlfriend, I'm going to find him a wife!" she'd say and continue to mail random photos and phone numbers to Brandon so he could pass them along. Which he never did. Except this time, he actually considered it. His friend seemed to be in some kind of dating slump. It had been months since he'd brought a woman to the restaurant or even talked about meeting one.

Dante blamed his dry spell on work. And for right now, Brandon accepted the excuse because he had more pressing things to worry about than whether his friend was getting laid on a regular basis.

They'd reached Dante's office and he motioned for Brandon to take a seat on one of the leather chairs next to his desk.

"Lorena is always watching out for me, isn't she? Please tell her that I'm praying for her," Dante said as he sat down across from him.

"I will. Thank you, my friend."

Silence fell between them, as if neither wanted to bring up why Brandon had been forced to stop at Dante's office, before heading in to the restaurant.

Finally, Dante cleared his throat. "So…did you see it?"

"Nope. Show me."

Brandon watched as Dante pulled a manila envelope out of his top desk drawer. He handed it to Brandon. "Who is she?"

Brandon sighed and opened the envelope. "She's an event planner I work with sometimes. Her cousin owns Robles' Panaderia and…son of a bitch!"

It was a hard copy of an article from one of the online tabloid websites. Brandon didn't even look at the article and instead focused on the photo right above it. The fuzzy, yet discernible, image of him and Daisy making out in front of her hotel room door ignited a blaze of emotions within him. Desire, rage, frustration—they all boiled to the surface. The invasion of privacy was beyond reprehensible. What happened between him and Daisy that night was one of the most intimate moments that could happen between two people. And now some fucking tabloid had cheapened it.

In the two years since the restaurant had been featured on a few national TV shows, he'd been the target of more than one paparazzi attack. He usually didn't care when he was met with a barrage of flashes after leaving a nightclub. If people were talking about him, they were talking about the restaurant, too. And the women on his arm enjoyed the attention. Hell, some of them probably dated him just for the chance of being photographed.

But this was different. *Daisy* was different. And he felt violated for her.

He couldn't bear to look at it anymore. He shoved it back into the envelope and tossed it back to Dante. "Who took it?"

"The editor wouldn't tell me. The article's source is a hotel employee so I got my hands on employment and social security records and there's one name that stands out."

"Who is it?"

"Felipe Campos."

"Fuck!" Brandon roared and stood up, unable to contain his rage any longer. Felipe Campos was a piece of shit former employee who'd swindled the restaurant—and Alex—then sued for wrongful termination when they let him go. "It has to be him. But how? I mean I would've seen…" Then it hit him—Daisy's warning that someone had been watching them in the hallway.

"I'm actually surprised he didn't contact you or me first," Dante said. "You'd think he'd try to get you to pay him for the photos."

Brandon shook his head. "No. This was about revenge.

When the judge threw out his lawsuit, he threatened that he'd find a way to get back at me. This way, he gets some money out of it, too."

"Really? You think he's that pissed off?"

"Come on Dante. I've been in Puerto Rico for two weeks. Why didn't the story break a few days ago? No, he somehow made sure all hell would break loose when I got back to town. My sister really knows how to pick them, huh?"

"I'm trying to keep my mouth shut when it comes to your sister's exes. But this guy gives scumbags a bad name."

"Maybe I should've just paid him to get out of our lives."

"He only would've come back and demanded double," Dante explained. "Guys like this don't disappear once they get a taste of free money."

It still gnawed at him that he'd been the one to bring Felipe into the restaurant in the first place. The guy had everyone fooled, including Alex, in the beginning. Besides cheating on his sister, it turned out he'd also been cheating the restaurant by paying himself extra through forged invoices. When Brandon threatened to call the police, Felipe threatened to drag his sister through a sexual harassment lawsuit, since she'd technically been his boss when they had started dating. So Brandon fired him and made sure no one in the industry would ever hire him again. Felipe tried to sue him anyway. Thank God the judge had seen right through it.

"Brandon, there's more." Dante's serious tone shook him out of his thoughts.

"What else could there fucking be?"

"You didn't read the article. In it, the unnamed hotel employee supposedly has proof that you and Daisy were secretly married two weeks ago."

He couldn't hold in the laughter if he tried. The tension he'd been feeling just a few seconds ago evaporated. There was no way Felipe could prove he and Daisy were married.

Dante looked at him with squinty eyes. "I'm glad you find this so funny."

Brandon caught his breath. "Sorry, man. It's just the most ridiculous thing in the world. Me? Married? I don't know what so-called proof Felipe has, but I can assure you there is nothing that proves I got married two weeks ago. I attended a friend's wedding, and I hooked up with the maid of honor. End of story."

"Really? I mean, I kind of thought it was farfetched. At least, I hoped I'd be one of the first ones to know if you decided to tie the knot."

"Trust me, my friend," he said, still smiling. "You would be, because I'd be calling you almost immediately to file my divorce papers."

Dante visibly relaxed. "Well, good. I feel better now. I'm assuming you want me to call the tabloid and demand a retraction?"

"And add that if they don't, you'll be filing lawsuit papers tomorrow."

"What about Daisy?"

The mention of her name stilled him. "What about her?"

"Do I need to contact her and get her to sign the standard non-disclosure agreement? Felipe may not have a story to sell, but if you two spent the night together then it's best if we lock it down now."

He almost laughed out loud again. Sleeping on the couch in her hotel room wasn't exactly spending the night together. "No need. We don't have to worry about Daisy going to the tabloids, too."

"Are you sure?"

He was sure. There wasn't any story to tell. At least not one that the tabloids would be interested in. "She's a friend. No non-disclosure agreement."

"If you think that's best…" Dante pulled the article out

of the envelope again and fed it to the shredder next to his desk.

He'd been friends with Dante too long not to notice the tone behind his words. "I *do* think that's best, but it sounds like you don't."

Dante shrugged. "I'm just the lawyer. What do I know?"

"Spill it."

"Look, as your lawyer I'll give you all the legal advice I can," he continued. "And as your friend, I'll give you all the personal advice you'll let me. Either way, it's up to you whether you take it or not."

It wasn't the first time he'd done something without listening to Dante's advice. And so far, everything had worked out just fine. He already owned two very successful restaurants and was working hard on a third. When it came to business, his gut of steel never steered him wrong.

In fact, if he'd listened to his gut the night of Amara's wedding instead of another part of his anatomy, there'd be no photo or article at all.

"Look, I get that you're just watching out for me. But I can trust Daisy. She's not the sort of girl who would sell me out like that. No matter what happened between us."

Dante nodded. "I guess you're right. Besides, she's probably just as pissed at seeing herself plastered all over the internet this morning."

And that's when Brandon's so-called steel gut flinched.

Chapter Four

So this is what an over-steamed zucchini feels like.

Daisy walked out of The Quiet Soul yoga studio with soggy clothes and limp body parts. The twenty or so feet to her car might as well have been five hundred. When she finally made it, she flopped onto the front seat and guzzled down her third bottle of water. Yep, her first class of extreme hot yoga would definitely be her last.

She had wanted to try it ever since the studio began offering it a few weeks ago, but she usually arrived too late for the sold-out 7:30 a.m. class. Today, though, she'd set every alarm in her apartment in order to make sure she'd get up on time for the class others had described to her as "an invigorating experience."

Invigorating? My sweat-soaked ass it is.

What a fool she had been. Yoga was already hard enough. Why on the earth had anyone wanted to make it life threatening, too?

Daisy sat behind the wheel for a few minutes trying to cool down, but it didn't work. She needed to turn on the A/C but even reaching out to turn on the ignition seemed beyond her capabilities at that moment. Then her yoga bag buzzed with another dilemma.

It was sitting *all the way* across the car on the passenger seat. Getting it would involve stretching her body and she was *so* done with stretching.

What if it's a potential customer? You'll kick yourself if you don't answer.

Daisy heaved her arm toward her bag and pulled out her cell phone. "Please be someone who can bring me more water and turn on the car for me," she groaned after seeing an unfamiliar number on the display screen.

"Hello," she said with more energy than she felt.

"Can I speak with Daisy?" a man's voice replied.

"This is she. How can I help you?"

"Hi Daisy. My name is Oliver and I'm doing a follow-up article to the story that ran today on the Gossip Town website about your secret wedding to L.A. Cuchara owner Brandon Montoya. Is it true he made you sign a pre-nup?"

Her phone slipped out of her grasp from either shock or her clammy hand. She quickly picked it up off her lap, wiped the sweat off with the hem of her T-shirt and put it back against her ear. "Whoa there. Who did you say you were again? What article?"

The man sighed. "I'm Oliver Jones, a reporter with the online entertainment website Gossip Town. Didn't you see the article we ran today about you and your new husband?"

Even if she had ever heard of the site, she'd been too busy drowning in her own perspiration to go online this morning. "No, I didn't see it. And I don't know what you think you know, but I'm not married to Brandon Montoya."

"I have a copy of the reservation form for the honeymoon suite at the Hotel Esperanza and a copy of the banquet and catering statement that say otherwise."

"That was my cousin's wedding, idiot. Of course all of the paperwork is going to have my name on it because I was the freaking wedding planner. And I'm pretty positive that nowhere on that paperwork does it say that I'm the one that got married that day or that I married Brandon."

"Uh-huh. I see. Can I quote you on that?"

"Yes, you can quote me on that and then you can shove that same quote right up your ass," she yelled and hung up.

Her phone buzzed again and she swiped it to answer without looking at the number. "Call me again and I'll show you exactly what it means to suffer for your art."

"What art? Why are you yelling at me?"

"Amara! Oh my God. I'm so sorry. I thought you were this nasty reporter. You'll never guess what happened."

"People think you married Brandon."

"People think— Wait, you know?"

"Irma from next door showed me the article. Guess the party continued after we left the hotel, huh? I didn't realize he could be so, um, handsy?"

"What are you talking about?"

"There's a picture with the article, Daisy. It shows you two going at it in one of the hotel hallways."

The satisfaction that she hadn't been paranoid about someone watching them that night was overshadowed by her sheer embarrassment. She didn't have to look in her rearview mirror to know that her face, already warm from the yoga, burned even redder.

Daisy covered her eyes with her free hand. "I'm sorry, Amara. I was planning on telling you. But I wanted to wait until you came back from Hawaii."

"We've been back for three days and I've seen you for two of them. What happened? You don't even *like* him!"

This conversation was making her sweat all over again. She turned on the ignition and blasted the air. "I didn't," she said with a sigh as she held her face close to one of the vents. "I don't, I mean. Well, not really. But I asked him to kiss me to make stupid Luis jealous and we did some tequila shots and it's a long story that I'd rather not go into over the phone. I'll come over and we can talk."

"Fine. But you might want to wait a while before heading over. There's some guy who keeps coming in to buy coffee and *pan dulce*. I think he's looking for you. Maybe he's that reporter who called you."

"Ugh. Maybe. All right, call me when the coast is clear."

"Okay. So what are you going to do?"

"Right now? Well, I'm going to try to drive myself home without passing out, then I'm going to wring out the clothes I'm wearing and eventually take a very long and very cold shower. Then I'm going to head over to L.A. Cuchara. Brandon is supposed to be back from Puerto Rico today, and I think it's time for me and my new husband to have a little chat."

Chapter Five

God, could this day get any worse?

Brandon examined the crinkled corner of his five-month-old Jaguar's back fender and resisted the urge to utter every single curse word he knew in English and in Spanish. He was parked in the alleyway behind L.A. Cuchara, but it was lunchtime, and he could see people already gathering on the sidewalk as they waited for an open table. He didn't want to cause a scene—he'd already done that outside the bank after the other car ran into him while he was pulling out of the parking space. The other driver had the nerve to blame him for not paying attention even though the guy still clutched his phone in his hand while waving and screaming at Brandon. He'd lost it and screamed right back. It wasn't until the police showed up that he finally calmed down.

But now after inspecting the damage up close, he became riled up all over again. What in the world had he done to deserve such a shitty day?

After leaving Dante's office, he'd gotten a phone call from his Miami contractor saying the city planners had pulled his restaurant proposal from the agenda of the next council meeting because of "issues" that had been raised in an independent traffic study. It was just another delay in a long list of bumps and detours he'd had to deal with over the past year, trying to get final approval to start renovations on the Miami Beach property he purchased with the intention of opening up his third restaurant—Miami Cuchara.

He'd been at the bank because he'd tried to use his personal credit card last night at the airport but it was declined. Someone had stolen the account information and had been on a spending spree back in Puerto Rico. It had taken him two hours to get everything straightened out.

The car accident had been the bitter topping on a pretty fucked up day.

He let out a frustrated growl and forced himself to walk away from the car before he dented it somewhere else with his fist. Stomping through the kitchen, he was grateful the staff knew well enough to stay out of his way. And after a few quick strides, he made it into his office without having to deal with another catastrophe. He slammed the door behind him and collapsed onto his desk chair.

I need a drink. No, scratch that, I need drinks. *As in, multiple.*

He was just about to stand up and head for the restaurant bar when his cell phone buzzed in his pants pocket.

What now? He pulled it out and glanced at the screen. Concern melted his anger as he wondered why his mother was calling him at eleven thirty on a Tuesday morning.

"Hello, *Mamá*. Is everything okay?

"No, everything is not okay! It's bad enough I have the cancer but now you want to give me a heart attack, too?"

His worry lessened. Her usual dramatics meant she wasn't likely calling about a life or death emergency. No, she was more passive aggressive on those topics. He usually had to pull them out of her after she'd already insisted all was fine. So the fact that she was giving him a guilt trip meant he'd done something he didn't even know about, and he'd just have to let her go on and on until he apologized for whatever it was she thought he did.

He leaned back into his chair and closed his yes. "Take a breath, *Mamá. Cálmate.*"

"No me puedo calmar."

"Why can't you calm down? Why are you so upset?"

"Tell me, Brandon. Am I bad mother?"

"Of course not, *Mamá.*" He sighed.

"Then why, *mijo?* Why did I have to find out from a stranger *que eres casado?*"

Brandon's eyes flew open and he sat straight up in his chair. "Married? *Mamá,* who told you I was married?"

"The computer. Beatrice's daughter see it and tell her, and Beatrice come over and show to me."

Fury surged up from his belly and up his neck, strangling him like a noose. He had to loosen his tie and unbutton his collar. "*Mamá,* how many times have I told you that you can't always believe what you read on those kind of websites?"

"Yes, I know, *mijo.* I tell Beatrice that's not possible. I tell her I would know if my son has a wife. But the picture! Tell me it's not true, Brandon. *Por favor,* tell me you didn't stay here for two weeks in my house while your new wife stay hiding in Los Angeles. Is it because she already don't like me? Did you tell her I was a bad mother, is that why she no want to meet me?"

"*Mamá,* please slow down. Let me explain before you really do have a heart attack."

"Maybe I am already. My heart is beating too fast in my chest. After Beatrice left I have to sit down because I couldn't breathe. Your cousin Tomas is already looking on the computer so he can buy me a ticket tonight to come to Los

Angeles."

His own heart sped up. "Wait. You're coming to Los Angeles? But why?"

"To meet your wife!"

"So let me get this straight. I begged and pleaded with you for two weeks to fly back with me so I could get you an appointment with a cancer specialist, but you refused. But now, all of a sudden, you're ready to get on a plane just to meet Daisy?"

"Is that her name? Daisy? This is what I mean, *mijo*. This woman is now my daughter and I don't even know her name. Of course I'm coming to Los Angeles. I need to know my new daughter and make her see I'm not such a terrible mother. I already asked *Señora* Ruiz to water my plants while I'm gone, and *Señor* Bustamante is going to take over my Sunday shift at the food kitchen, and I'm going to have to cancel my…"

Brandon waited for her take a breath so he could interrupt and tell her the truth about Daisy. But the more he listened to her go on and on, the more he realized that once she knew there wasn't a real daughter-in-law to meet, there was no way she'd be getting on a plane.

The knot of helplessness in the pit of his stomach tightened—he'd had it since learning she'd been diagnosed with cervical cancer. Within a couple of hours of their conversation, he'd called everyone he could think of and asked for the name of the best oncologist in the city. One of his customers, a pharmaceutical rep, helped him get a phone call with one of the doctors on staff at the USC Norris Comprehensive Cancer Center. He'd agreed to see his mother and review her plan of care if she came to town. So Brandon had flown to Puerto Rico the day after Amara's wedding determined not to come back unless his mother was in the seat next to him. But after two weeks of begging, she'd still refused.

Although she blamed her busy volunteer schedule, there was another reason why she wouldn't come back with him. And he felt guilty as hell for it. He knew she saw her cancer as an imposition—something that could disrupt the life he'd worked so hard to build away from her and Puerto Rico. That was why she limited her phone calls to twice a week and why she'd only visited him once since he'd moved to L.A.

And why she'd waited over a month to tell him she was sick.

Brandon wanted to scream. What good was all of his money and all his success if he couldn't use it to help his *mamá* when she needed him the most? Maybe she preferred to fight this fight alone, but there was absolutely no way in this world that he was going to let her.

Too bad he wasn't really married, or even engaged.

An idea thundered into Brandon's head, drowning out the rest of what his mother was saying. It was a long shot, and even crazier than him pretending to be Daisy's boyfriend on the night of the wedding.

But what if Daisy pretended to be his fiancée?

The more he thought about it, the more he was convinced that this was his only option. Of course, it would only work if Daisy agreed to the plan. He had to talk to her about the tabloid story anyway. Might as well throw in a fake engagement, too.

He'd do whatever it took to convince her to go along with his plan. He just needed to get his mom on a plane as soon as possible.

"*Mamá.*" He attempted to stop her rambling. "*Mamá,* please, let me say something."

But she wouldn't let him get in a word between all of hers. So he had no choice but to yell: "*Mamá!* I'm not married! I'm engaged!"

Silence and then a hiss. "*Que?*"

"I'm trying to tell you that Daisy isn't my wife. She's my fiancée. That photo is from the night I asked her to marry me."

"But why you no tell me?"

"I'm sorry. I know I should have. But you'd just told me about the cancer, and I wanted you to focus on getting better. So if you think you're really up for a trip, why don't you still come to L.A. and meet your future daughter-in-law."

"*Aye, mijo!* This makes me so happy! I should still pinch you for not telling me when you were here but I'm glad I didn't miss your wedding. *Que buena!* Have you set a date yet?"

"No, *Mamá*. There's still so much to plan. How about I buy you a one-way ticket for next week? That way you can spend time with Daisy and maybe even see the doctor I told you about. What do you say?"

There was silence on the other end of the phone. And for a second, Brandon feared she'd still refuse. Then he heard her take a breath. "Okay, *mijo*, I'll come. I can't wait to meet her."

For the first time in weeks, the knot started to loosen. "I can't wait for you to meet her, too. You're going to love her, *Mamá*. Daisy is the most beautiful, generous, kindest woman I've ever—"

"Just who in the hell do you think you are?

Brandon nearly jumped out of his skin at the sound of Daisy's voice. She stood in his doorway, looking completely pissed off. He didn't have to guess why.

"Uh, *Mamá*?" he said into the phone. "I'm going to have to call you back."

• • •

Daisy waited as Brandon finished the call with his mother. She'd felt a twinge of regret about the way she'd stormed into his office once she realized to whom he was talking to. But she pushed it down, determined to stay mad so she could tell him off the way she'd practiced during the drive over.

She wasn't sure what angered her more—the fact that she'd been ambushed by this article or the fact that seeing him again had rustled up feelings she wasn't prepared to face just yet.

"God help me— No. God help *you* if you knew anything about this article coming out," she told him once he put his phone down.

He waved his hands. "I swear I didn't. I just found out this morning."

"How did they get that photo, Brandon?"

"Why don't you take a seat first? You're making me nervous standing there like that."

"I'll sit when I want to sit. Start talking."

"There's this ex-employee of mine named Felipe Campos—"

"And what? He somehow managed to be at the same hotel where we, where we almost…"

"Yes. My lawyer found out he works there now."

Daisy's stomach fell. "The guy with the cart?"

"The guy with the cart."

"I don't understand. How can you be so calm about this?"

"Because we both know the story's not true. Well, what the photo shows is true, but there's no proof that we're married. My lawyer has already called the editor demanding a retraction."

Although she still wanted to be angry, Daisy had to admit that Brandon had a point. All the photo showed was a couple making out. There was no story there.

But as the cloud of anger hovering over her dissipated, the bumblebees attacked. Almost sleeping with him hadn't calmed the hive, it had only aggravated it. "Fine. I guess. But if anything else comes up, you better call me."

"I will. And I'm sorry you got dragged into this mess. Felipe is after me, not you."

She nodded and turned to walk away, but he called her name. The look on his face worried her. "What? Is there video, too?"

He shook his head. "No, but there is another issue we have to discuss. And maybe you should sit down for this one."

His tone and his eyes told her that she should indeed take a seat. "Brandon, you're freaking me out. Spill it."

"Well, it turns out that we weren't the only ones upset by the article."

"Shit. Did Amara call you, too?"

"Amara? No. I'm talking about my mother. I had just finished calming her down when you walked in."

Even though she didn't know Brandon's mother, the thought of her—or any mother—seeing those photos enflamed her cheeks. "Oh. So she saw—"

"Yeah. It's actually more complicated than that. Remember I told you that she has cancer?"

Daisy's chest tightened. She could see the worry on his face, and she felt for him.

"Yes, I remember. But what does that have to do with the article?"

"While we were in Puerto Rico, my sister and I tried to convince her to come to Los Angeles and see a specialist at USC. But no matter what we did or said, she refused to come here. That is until today, when she thought we were married."

"I'm still not understanding. You told her we weren't, though, right?"

"I did."

"Okay, so what's the issue?"

"The issue is I need to get her to Los Angeles and the only way to get her here is to…"

"To what?"

"Daisy, will you pretend to be my fiancée?"

Had she been standing, she would've fallen into the chair. Instead she gripped the armrests. "I'm sorry. I thought you just asked me to—"

"To marry me, or rather, pretend that you're going to marry me. Just for a few weeks while she's in town."

She gripped the chair harder, only to keep herself from falling out of it. "No."

"No?"

"No. I won't pretend to be your fiancée."

"But why not? I pretended to be your boyfriend."

"Oh. My. God. That is so not the same. I'm not lying to your mother. You'll just have to find another way to get her here."

"There is no other way. Believe me, I've tried. The only thing that can get her on a plane is the promise of meeting her future daughter-in-law, and that's you."

"But it's not me." She couldn't believe they were having this conversation. In fact, *no one* would believe they were having this conversation.

"I'll pay you, of course. Just name your price."

That's when the anger returned. Daisy jumped to her feet. "Why is it *always* about money with you? I'm not for sale. Good-bye, Brandon."

She heard him get up from his desk and before she reached the door, he grabbed her hand. Flashbacks of their exchange that night in the hotel lobby tackled her and she released a breath.

"I never meant to imply that, Daisy. Please, just hear me out."

Against her better judgment, she didn't punch him in the gut. Instead she watched him release her hand and then push his office door closed.

"Look, Brandon, I'm sorry about your mother. But this is

kind of a major thing you're asking. It's not just lying to her over the phone. Once she's here, it takes it to a whole other level. And given our recent history, I just don't think I'm the right girl for you—for this."

"But that's the thing, Daisy. You are *absolutely* the perfect girl for this. You just have to look at this like another business partnership. And because of our history, we know we're compatible. We're obviously attracted to each other, so we don't have to pretend there. And, like you said, we're friends."

"Don't you have other *friends* who could do this? What about that redhead you were dating last month, or the Victoria's Secret model you were supposed to take to Amara's wedding?"

His eyebrows shot up. "I didn't realize you were keeping tabs on my dating life."

Whoops. "Please. Don't flatter yourself. I'm just making the point that your so-called dating life is public knowledge. So why don't you just ask one of those girls to do this. I bet there's a wannabe actress in your harem who would jump at the chance to be your fiancée—pretend or otherwise."

"That's the problem. Once you have a romantic relationship with someone, you can't call them up and ask them to go down that path again. Sure, you and I almost slept together, but that wasn't about being in a real relationship. It was about sex. That's it. And when we realized we were making a mistake, we stopped. This is why it needs to be you. I need someone who can draw the line between emotion and practicality. I need you, Daisy."

The shock of his request began to die down. It still was too much to comprehend. Pretend to be engaged to Brandon? There was no way.

"Just hear me out before you say something." He could read her like a label. She really had no poker face. "My dad died when I was just a kid. My mom and Alex are the only real family I have left in this world, and I can't just sit by and do nothing. I know this plan is beyond ridiculous, but it's the only plan I've got. I don't know what else to do. All I need is two weeks. Please."

He was grabbing her hand again—clenching it, actually. Her breath caught in her chest once she allowed herself to look into his eyes. She'd never seen Brandon so exposed. His pain was palpable, and she ached for him.

She imagined what she would do if the tables were turned. What if it were her father who had cancer and the only way she could be certain he was getting the treatment he needed was to ask Brandon to be her fiancé? The magnitude of the request finally hit home. But the little voice issued one more warning.

He's just using you to get something he wants. Just like the night of Amara's wedding. And when he gets it, you'll be nothing to him again.

Maybe. But could she really continue their professional relationship knowing she hadn't helped him? Could he? When it came down to it, Daisy didn't see any other choice. The only thing she could do was to make sure she got something out of the deal—something to ensure she walked away with her pride and business plan intact.

"Fine. I'll do it."

His whole body deflated in relief and he let go of her hand. She quickly dismissed the tinge of disappointment. "Thank you so much, Daisy," he said. "You have no idea what this means to me."

"Yeah, well, before you start thanking me, don't you want to know what it's going to cost you?"

"I thought you said…"

"I still don't want money."

"Then what?"

"I want you to introduce me to Christian Santos and his

fiancée Mira."

She waited for him to protest, or worse, laugh again. He did neither. "You've got a deal."

"Really?"

"Really. You know I can't guarantee anything. I'll make the introduction, but the rest will be up to you."

"I know. I know. Don't worry."

His eyebrow lifted. "You sound pretty confident. I'll have to warn you, though. Christian may act like a playboy on the small screen but he's not one in real life. Since he met Mira he hasn't so much as glanced at another woman."

She put her fists on her hips. "Well, that's original. You think I'm going to flirt my way into getting a job? I'd be offended if it weren't so ridiculous. You really don't know me, do you?"

And why did it matter so much?

"I stand corrected," he told her. "What's your plan then?"

"Mira. My plan is Mira."

"I don't understand."

"Of course you don't. That's the point. You can't understand something you know nothing about." She waved her hands at his lavish office. "Mira isn't a celebrity like you or Christian. She's a regular girl who was living a regular life until a famous person fell in love with her. If my instincts are correct, Mira isn't going to want a big Hollywood wedding or a big Hollywood wedding planner. She's going to want a regular girl like her."

"Daisy, you are many things. But a *regular* girl is not one of them," he said with a very telling smile.

Somewhere during her tirade, he'd grabbed her hand again. She hadn't realized it until the moment his thumb grazed hers. It triggered a familiar ache between her thighs. A frustrating consequence of coming so close to, well, *coming* with Brandon. God, she better not be wearing her unwanted arousal on her face. The last thing she needed was to let him know that he'd flipped a switch within her.

Too late. He stepped closer and his eyes raked over her body. It might as well have been his tongue, given the way her nipples pebbled in response.

"You know, just because we're going to be pretending to be engaged doesn't mean we have to pretend other things," he said, his voice low and teasing.

Her pulse quickened. "Really? Like what things exactly?"

"Like right now. I don't have to pretend that I haven't been able to forget kissing those sweet, soft lips of yours. And you don't have to pretend that you don't want me to kiss them again." He moved even closer to her, the space between them so small that the heat of his breath fanned her cheeks.

The abrupt change in his body language and tone threw her for a loop. Her mind raced, trying to figure what had caused him to go from zero to horny in just a few seconds. They'd just made a business agreement, and usually those didn't require a make-out session to seal the deal. Perhaps he was testing her to see if she could act like a smitten fiancée?

That had to be it. It was time to show him that she could get physical without getting emotional—just like him.

"Fine. Let's stop pretending then." His shocked eyes were the last thing she saw before she pulled him down by his jacket lapels and smashed her lips against his. It was a hard and fast kiss—meant more to be a statement than an invitation—but before she could bask in having caught him off guard, he turned the tables and pulled her back in for more. The gruffness gave way to passion, and before she knew it, he was arching her backward over his desk, one arm bracing her shoulders and the other encircling her waist.

Her body was on fire, his tongue the accelerant. And God help her, she wanted to combust beneath him.

A knock on the door saved her from such a fate.

"Excuse me Mr. Montoya," a man's voice said from the other side, "but there's a problem with today's seafood order. We need you to come talk to the vendor."

"I'll be right there," he yelled after breaking the kiss. Pulling her back up, he gave her a quick peck and walked to the other side of his desk. She straightened her hair and clothes. What the hell had just happened? A few minutes ago she had been ready to strangle him. If they hadn't been interrupted, who knows what she would've done instead.

She watched him as he picked up some papers and his cell phone. "So, did I pass your stupid test?"

"What test?" he asked without looking at her.

"The one to see if I could act like a fiancée. I mean, I don't expect you to manhandle me like that in public, but at least you know I'll be, um, receptive."

He laughed, yet his eyes were serious. "You thought that was a test?"

"Of course. Why else would I kiss you, and why else would you kiss me back…like that?"

"I don't know why you kissed me, but I kissed you because you are a goddamn sexy woman and I can't stop wondering what it would be like to finally see you naked."

His directness stirred something deep inside her. No man had ever said anything like that to her. Ever.

On cue, the tiny, nagging voice inside her head reminded her of the reality of the situation.

This isn't a real relationship, and it won't ever be one. Sex with Brandon would only complicate things.

She cleared her throat. "I appreciate your frankness. So I'll be just as honest. It's obvious we're attracted to each other, and while I'm sure the sex would be amazing, I still think it would be a mistake to give in to our, um, desires. You said it yourself. We have to think of this as a business deal."

"So our arrangement should be a platonic one?"

"Yes. Is that okay?" she rushed.

"Well, of course it's okay, Daisy. I'm not a brute who's going to force you into my bed. You're doing a huge favor for me, and I'm willing to respect and follow your terms of negotiation."

Relief washed over her, taking the last embers of that fiery kiss with it. "Good. Thank you."

"Before we shake on it, though, I do have one more request given our mutual agreement to keep this platonic."

Why did she already think she'd have an issue with this next request? "Well? Spill it."

"I think you should move in with me while my mom's here."

Alarm bells sounded off inside her head. "I thought you just said you were willing to keep things rated PG?"

"Hold up. I never said PG. How about PG-13?"

"Brandon…"

He laughed and went over to her. "Okay, we'll discuss ratings later. But hear me out about the living together situation. As much as I think the story about us will die down eventually, what if the paparazzi continue to dig for a new one? What if they start following you home?"

Daisy thought about the man at the bakery that Amara had mentioned. Instead of feeling afraid, she got pissed off. "I know how to take care of myself. I've been doing it since I was a kid."

He raised his eyebrow at her comment. "I'm sure you can. But at least if you stay with me, I can protect your privacy. The gated entrance and security kiosk pretty much guarantee that no one will walk up to the door just to ask you questions or take more photos."

Although she hated to admit it, the idea of camping out at Brandon's while this story died down seemed like a good one. Except for one major detail. "What about sleeping arrangements?"

He didn't hesitate. "You can take the master and I'll sleep in the guest bedroom. Both are upstairs. My mom has a bad knee and can't climb stairs very well so she won't be making any surprise visits. Plus, you know I'm always here at the restaurant anyway. Unless we plan to do something with my mom together, I bet we'll barely see each other."

Living in Brandon's house, sleeping in a room next to his, and hanging out with his mother seemed like an alternate reality she wasn't quite ready to cross into. Could she really go through with it?

Brandon didn't notice her apprehension and stepped even closer. "However, in the spirit of being as transparent as possible, I do need to let you know that I'll always be willing to renegotiate the terms of our agreement. If you know what I mean?"

She rolled her eyes and folded her arms across her chest. "I'll always know what you mean. But that's not going to happen. Sorry."

"Whatever you say," he said and opened the door for her. "Just as long as you at least act like you want to sleep with me when my mom is around."

"Ewww."

Brandon's cheeks reddened. "You know what I mean."

And for the first time that day, she laughed. But her amusement disappeared as another thought entered her mind.

"Speaking of parents… If your mom saw that article then there's a good chance my dad will have, too. I need to go talk to him."

"What are you going to say?"

Daisy thought for a moment. What could she say? Would her dad understand why she would agree to take part in such an elaborate charade? What if he didn't? Either way she couldn't ask him to lie, too. She had to protect him.

"I'll tell him we're getting married."

His eyes widened. "By yourself? You don't have to, you know. I could do it with you."

She shook her head and sighed. "For your own safety, it's best that you not be there."

"Seriously? You really don't want me to meet your dad?"

"Not yet. Let's just see how things go, okay?"

...

Later, as she drove to the bakery, Daisy replayed everything that happened in Brandon's office. It still didn't seem real. How had she ended up pretending to be in love with a man who changed girlfriends as often as his ties? Her life had definitely taken a strange turn since Amara's wedding.

Hopefully, it would be for the better.

Except she hated that she had to get her dad mixed up in the craziness. But it was a small price to pay for getting her event planning business off the ground and getting her life back on track. Her dad had given up so much to raise her on his own and send her off to an expensive college. And how did she repay him? By quitting her high-paying marketing job last year so she could figure out her real passion.

He'd been angry when he finally found out she'd left the agency on her own. To him, work was all about getting a paycheck. Passion and personal fulfillment had nothing to do with it. If you didn't like your job, so what? Unless you could find a better one, you just kept doing it. Thirty years in a factory had taught him that.

It had been the first time he'd ever told her that he was disappointed in her.

The event planning business was the chance she needed to prove to herself—and to him—that she hadn't made the worst mistake of her life.

But now there was the little issue of her fake engagement…

Maybe she could get through the next two weeks without having to introduce him to Brandon. Eventually she'd tell her dad that the engagement had been called off, that they'd rushed into things and realized they didn't love each other.

Her dad should be relieved that she didn't end up marrying someone who was so wrong for her. In the end, he might even understand.

That was the best-case scenario. The worst-case? Well, she didn't even want to think of it.

Chapter Six

Brandon checked his watch again. It was only ten minutes later than the last time he looked. His mom's plane was scheduled to land in less than an hour. Which meant he had less than sixty minutes left of being a bachelor.

Shouldn't he being doing something, anything, to mark the occasion?

He glanced around his office and sighed. Unless there was a stripper holding an expensive bottle of whiskey about to burst through the door, Brandon would have to settle with toasting good-bye to the single life with the iced tea he'd been nursing since lunch.

"To me," he said sarcastically, and took a drink.

Then the door opened, and for a second he wondered how the universe had known.

"Oh, good, you're in here," Dante said as he walked inside.

Brandon could feel the blood draining from his face. "Damn, Dante," he muttered.

His friend stopped in the middle of his office. "But I haven't even told you yet."

He'd been prepared to tease Dante a little more about ruining his last hour as a single man, but his words made him realize there was nothing funny about why he had shown up. It had to be about the Miami project.

"What happened now?" he groaned.

"The project manager heard from a friend at another construction company that the city is thinking of rezoning."

"How can the city do that? *Why* would they do that?"

"The other company just bid on a possible redevelopment project for the city. Based on the initial plans, the city would purchase that vacant lot down the street from the restaurant site and lease it to a private developer who wants to build condos on it. If they do that, then that means—"

Brandon shook his head in disbelief. "That block would become a residential zone and I wouldn't be able to sell any alcohol at the restaurant."

Dante took a seat across the desk from him. "Nothing is for sure yet. The team called me because they wanted to find out what the legal issues were before telling you. I have some thoughts, but I plan to keep researching. In the meantime, I figured it was better that you know now."

It *was* better. Though not by much. This wasn't the kind of news he needed just before he was going to go see his mom. But knowing Dante was on top of the situation would help him push it aside for now. He trusted his friend, trusted his expertise. If anyone could figure it out, it was him. He'd been the youngest person in his firm's history to make partner. That's why Brandon kept him on such a hefty retainer. It had nothing to do with friendship and everything to do with the fact that Dante knew his shit.

"I appreciate you telling me. This project is really becoming a giant pain in the ass, isn't it? Before you walked in, I was thinking of having a drink to mourn my bachelorhood. But now I may need to mourn this project instead. Son of a bitch."

"Ah, that's right. You're picking up Lorena today. Sorry, my friend. I didn't mean to ruin your day."

Brandon sighed. "Not your fault. It's been a weird day all around. Truth is, I'm having second thoughts."

"About your mom coming to L.A.?"

"No, not that. About asking Daisy to pretend to be my fiancée. My mom hasn't even landed yet and this charade is already becoming way more complicated than I thought it would be." Dante sighed and Brandon's ears burned. He knew that sigh well. "What? You know you're not technically going to be right until you tell me." Before Dante could answer, his sister rushed through the door. "You ready to go yet? I swear sometimes I think you like making me wait." Alex noticed he wasn't alone and stopped in her tracks. "Oh. Hey, Dante."

"Hey, Alexa." His friend gave her a curt nod. They stared at each other for a few seconds. The tension in the room shifted, and Brandon was both relieved and confused. Why did he always feel like a third wheel when it came to these two?

He stood up and grabbed his keys. "Sorry, didn't realize you were waiting for me. Dante had to fill me in on some stuff about the Miami project and, if I know him as well as I think I do, he was also just about to lecture me about this fake engagement with Daisy. Am I right, Dante?"

His friend shifted in his seat. But it was Alex who spoke. "Well, it's definitely not one of your brightest ideas, my brother."

His sister's comment made Dante chuckle, but not him.

"What do you mean? I thought you supported it?"

"I supported it because it got *Mami* on a plane and will get her in front of that oncologist tomorrow. That doesn't mean I don't think it's risky as hell—for both you and Daisy."

He didn't understand her sudden concern. "How is it risky? We're going into this with our eyes wide open. Everything will be fine."

Dante chuckled again. "Famous last words."

His sister rolled her eyes. "Look, all I'm saying is that it's not like you're going to be living with a troll for the next two weeks. Daisy is beautiful and smart and funny. The whole internet already knows you can't keep your hands off her, so you need to be prepared in case your perfect plan doesn't end up going the way you thought."

"I'm not going to deny that I'm attracted to her. And I'm not going to deny that it wouldn't be the worst thing in the world if we decided together to, uh, enjoy the physical benefits of being engaged. But even if that *does* happen, it still doesn't mean we can't walk away from this and go back to our normal lives."

Dante threw up his hands. "Seriously? What is it with you Montoyas and relationships? They don't all have to be based on just sex."

Alex whipped her head around to look at Dante. "Hey now. How did I get dragged into this? I'm not the one who asked someone to pretend to be in love with them."

"Please. Your relationships are just as fake as Brandon and Daisy's. At least she knows going in that it's all pretend."

"And just who in the hell gave you the right to judge my relationships? Last I heard, spending every night with your TiVo and takeout Chinese isn't a real relationship either."

"How would you know how I spend my nights? Last *I* heard, you didn't want to find out."

That was way more than he wanted to hear. Like always. Some days he felt like their referee. Other days, like today, he felt like their relationship counselor. He wasn't in the mood to be either. Brandon jumped up before Alex said something she'd regret. "Okay, guys. Cool it. I need to think."

They both mumbled an apology as he walked out of his office. He needed a few minutes alone to get his head back on straight. The next two weeks were going to be difficult enough just dealing with his mom's diagnosis. He couldn't afford to lose focus by worrying about possible side effects or complications from this fake engagement. And, anyway, it was too late to turn back now.

So he had to push forward and concentrate on making his plan succeed, just like every other business deal.

Failure was not an option.

Chapter Seven

While her son preferred to keep his feelings bottled up, Lorena Montoya let them flow wildly.

As soon as Brandon helped her out of his car, the large woman rushed toward Daisy, who had been waiting nervously on the front steps of the condo. Before she could even offer a polite greeting, strong, thick arms pulled her into a soft, ample chest.

"I'm so very happy to meet you," *Señora* Montoya gushed into her hair.

Daisy awkwardly patted her on the back. Uncomfortable with such an unabashed show of affection from someone who was practically a stranger, she looked over at Brandon for rescue. But he just stood by the car, grinning and shaking his head.

It wasn't until she finally pulled away that Daisy noticed the tears streaming down the woman's face.

Surprised by her own sudden emotions, she focused on getting into character. "It means so much to Brandon, to both of us, that you're here. Thank you for coming."

She looked again at Brandon, who was now smiling wildly and tilting his head in his mother's direction as if to signal that Daisy needed to do something more. So she plastered on a smile and gave the woman's hand a squeeze.

Señora Montoya laughed out loud. "The first thing you must know about me is that I'm a hugger, especially with my family." She reached and pulled Daisy into another hearty embrace. "Thank you for agreeing to marry my son. You have no idea how happy this makes me, *mija*. Oh, is it okay if I call you *mija*?"

No one but her father called her that, not even her own mother. Not that Daisy would've answered to it if she had ever tried. And it didn't feel right to let Lorena call her that either. Not when she knew she'd never be her daughter.

Daisy opened her mouth to respond but Brandon swooped in before she could. "*Mamá*, Daisy's very traditional. How about we wait for nicknames until after the wedding, okay?"

Señora Montoya nodded and smiled. This time the smile didn't reach her eyes, and Daisy knew the words had stung.

Guilt overwhelmed her and again she looked to Brandon for help. He wasn't grinning anymore either, and she knew he felt what she did. She cleared her throat and forced herself to sound cheery. "Well, it's going to be dark soon, so we better get you inside. I hope you're hungry. Alexa was here cooking up a storm before going to pick you up, since she has to work tonight at the restaurant."

Brandon grabbed the suitcases from the trunk and the three of them made their way into the condo. She guided *Señora* Montoya to the kitchen while he continued down the hallway to his mother's bedroom.

Daisy had officially moved in two days ago and had spent all her time since memorizing every nook and cranny in the place. It was a beautiful home with lots of natural light and high ceilings. Yet despite the physical warmth permeating through the tall windows, the space itself had seemed cold and unwelcoming when Daisy first walked in. It was sparsely furnished with no photos or knickknacks. Brandon said he'd lived there for nearly two years, yet it was as if he'd just moved in, too. That's when she realized the condo was a temporary home—a place for him to sleep and shower in between working at the restaurant and going out to clubs and parties. His mother would never believe that Daisy lived there, so with Alexa's help and Brandon's credit card, she'd added a woman's touch to the place, from flowers in the entryway to throw blankets on the leather couches. She'd even convinced Brandon to take a couple of photos with her that she then framed and displayed throughout the place. At the time she thought she might've gone overboard, but when his mother mentioned how much she liked one certain photo of them that she'd stuck to the refrigerator with a colorful magnet, Daisy knew it had all been worth it.

"Daisy, I love what you've done to the house," *Señora* Montoya said just as Brandon walked into the kitchen. "The last time I was here I felt like I stay at a hotel."

She laughed at her scrunched up expression and at Brandon's surprised one. "Thank you, *Señora* Montoya. But there's still a few more things I'd like to do."

"There are?" Brandon asked as he looked around.

"Oh yes. Don't worry, honey. You're going to love all the changes I have in store." She looked at him with a knowing smile.

"I'm sure I will…honey," he said, drawing out the endearment.

"Well, I can't wait to see it all, Daisy. Oh and please, call me Lorena. No need to be so formal when we are going to be family."

Family. It was such a simple word, yet it stirred up even

more complex emotions within her. She pushed them down again and then busied herself setting out plates and glasses for all three of them. Brandon brought out the trays of food that had been warming in the oven and they all sat at the table to eat.

About halfway through dinner, Daisy finally allowed herself to relax. Despite Brandon's warnings that his mother could be overbearing and bossy, Lorena had been nothing but pleasant and warm and funny. She'd even kept the questions to a minimum, asking only a few about Daisy's dad and her event planning business. Brandon must've warned her not to bring up the subject of Daisy's mom. He'd learned his lesson last night after pressing her for more details while they'd been cramming to make sure they knew enough about one another to pass as a couple in love.

And it was a good thing they'd studied, too. Because when dessert came out, so did the first test.

"*Mamá*, these cupcakes are from Daisy's cousin's bakery," Brandon said as he handed his mother one of Amara's famous *tres leches* cupcakes.

"How wonderful. That's where you two met, no?"

"Actually, we met at the restaurant," Daisy explained. "My cousin and I were there to try to convince Brandon and your daughter to put the bakery's desserts on the menu."

"That's right," Brandon added. "She actually hated me the first time we met."

Daisy nearly choked on a piece of cupcake. That wasn't the story they'd agreed to tell. The made-up story involved Brandon not wanting to let go of Daisy's hand when they were introduced and Daisy purposefully leaving her phone behind in the restaurant so she could see him later that night when they were supposed to have had their first kiss. What was Brandon doing?

"*Aye*, Brandon. I'm sure Daisy didn't hate you," Lorena

said with a laugh.

When she didn't agree, both of them looked at her. She met his eyes and saw the amusement. He was challenging her to tell the truth.

Would he ever learn?

"Well," she said and looked at his mother, "hate is such a strong word. I would say I didn't care for him…at all."

His mom laughed out loud. Satisfied with herself, Daisy licked caramel frosting off her fingers and smiled at Brandon.

"And I found her to be somewhat annoying," he said as he caught her gaze.

"Please," she said with a snort. "You were falling all over yourself trying to impress me."

Brandon shook his head. "More like I was trying to be nice to you, but you were making it very difficult with your nonstop eye rolls and exaggerated sighing."

The stress of the past few days boiled over. She'd been killing herself preparing to be the perfect fake fiancée and it was like he was purposefully trying to make her fail. From redecorating his house to learning how he liked his coffee, she'd done everything he'd asked and more. So why was he antagonizing her? Mother or not, she wasn't about to let him get away with his usual little digs.

"Of course I was rolling my eyes. You were going on and on about these special clams that were being flown in from Chile for dinner service that night. Clams. The way you talked about them… Dear Lord, it was like that plane was carrying the Pope instead of a bunch of seafood."

There went that jaw muscle again. "Do you know how hard it was to get those clams?" he said slowly.

"Actually, I do. Why? Because you kept telling me over and over again. Hence, the eye roll." She pointed to her right eye and looked up.

"Really, Daisy? I swear I—"

A voice interrupted their...whatever it was they were doing. "So when did your feelings change?"

She'd almost forgotten that Lorena was still there. They both turned to look at her at the same time. "Excuse me?" Daisy asked. "What?" Brandon said after.

Lorena clasped her hands and set them on the table. "When did your feelings turn into love?"

Daisy's heart pounded. Their cute fall-in-love story had been shredded into pieces once the floodgates opened about how they really felt about each other when they first met. There was no backup story to tell.

"*Mamá*..." Brandon warned. He must've sensed her panic

His mother looked at him with a wide-eyed innocence as fake as their couple photos on the fridge. "What? That's not too personal, is it? It's a simple question. Everyone knows that feeling and they can usually remember the moment it happened. I still remember exactly when I realized that your *papi* was the man I was going to marry."

Daisy's interest peaked. "You do?"

"*Pues*, of course. Those are the moments that you know your life will never be the same again."

She was definitely curious now—even a little jealous. What would it feel like to know that you had just met your soul mate?

Daisy had had her share of boyfriends over the years but she'd only used the "L" word with Luis. And even then it seemed like she had eased into it like a comfortable old shoe. There were no fireworks, no flashing Jumbotron messages that told her this was The Guy. No wonder it hadn't worked out.

"It's getting late, *Mamá*." Brandon's voice pulled her out of her thoughts. "How about we stop the interviewing for tonight, and you can ask her your questions later?"

Yeah, the conversation had taken a turn that she hadn't expected. "Brandon's right. You've had a long day and should rest," she told Lorena. "We have two whole weeks to get to know each other, right?"

Lorena patted Daisy's hand. "Or we can talk while I help you clean up?"

She gave Brandon another look. And he understood her unspoken message perfectly. "That's okay, *Mamá*. After I help you get settled, I'll come back and help Daisy. We love doing the dishes together, don't we, *sweetie*?"

Daisy nodded, only because if she opened her mouth she'd burst out laughing.

And when Brandon walked back into the kitchen a few minutes later asking to be put to work, she did just that.

"You're going to help me do dishes? You?"

"Sure. Why not?"

"Because you're *you*. You probably get more manicures than I do. I highly doubt those hands have ever been shriveled by dirty dishwater."

"Okay, first of all, I don't get manicures. Second of all, I'll have you know that my first job was as a dishwasher in my *tio's* restaurant back in Puerto Rico."

"What about now?"

"Now? Well, I use machines like everyone else."

"Oh really? So then how do you use this one? Because I've been staring at it for ten minutes and I still can't figure it out."

"Okay, well, only the housekeeper knows how to use this one. But that doesn't mean I don't remember how to scrub a pot."

"Fine then. You wash and rinse, and I'll dry and put away."

"Fine."

She watched as he unbuttoned his cuffs and rolled up his shirtsleeves. The tendons in his forearms flexed with the movement, and the memory of those strong arms around her made her inhale sharply, as if they were still tightening their grip on her. Daisy looked away before Brandon noticed she was staring and concentrated on finding a dishtowel. "Look, I'm sorry about saying that stuff about the clams and me not liking you very much when we first met." The corner of his mouth twitched and she relaxed. "It's just that you went off script and I didn't know how much I should say."

"So you said everything?"

"I said I was sorry."

He sighed and gave her a full smile. "I'm sorry, too. That was all my fault. From now on, we stick to the script, okay?"

"Okay." Part of her wanted to stay mad at him. That way she wouldn't notice just how damn sexy he looked lathering up a plate. She needed a distraction to keep herself from drooling all over the clean dishes.

"So, I didn't know you worked in your *tio's* restaurant. Is that what made you want to own one of your own?"

He nodded as he picked up another plate to wash. "Definitely. After my dad died, my mom started working there as a waitress. Then when Alex and I were old enough, we'd help out after school and on the weekends. I did everything from washing the dishes to mopping the floors to prepping the food. When we were in high school, that's when my *tio* finally let us cook. Alex loved being in the kitchen and finding ways to improve his recipes. But I always preferred being in the front of the house—the front of the restaurant. I liked seating the customers and checking in on them. I also started helping him run the business stuff, and that's when I knew what I wanted to do for the rest of my life."

"What made you leave, then? It sounds like you probably could've taken over your *tio's* restaurant and stayed in Puerto Rico."

"He did ask me to. His own kids were doing their own

thing and weren't interested. I almost said yes. I was going to skip college and just manage the restaurant full-time."

"So what changed your mind?"

"My mom did."

Daisy stopped drying the pan she was holding and turned to look at him. "She did? How?"

"When my dad died, everyone told me that I had to step up and take care of my mom and my sister. They told me I had to be the man of the house," he said matter-of-factly.

"How old were you?"

"Seven."

A familiar sense of loss rolled through her. "Wow. That's the same age I was when my mom left us."

They shared a knowing look before he turned back to scrub the inside of a glass. "I promised her at his funeral that I'd always take care of her and Alex. That's why I started working in the restaurant in the first place. I wanted to earn some money so I could help my *mamá* buy groceries and pay the bills. Then when I was older, I just figured she'd always need me around for something, so I didn't even let myself think about ever leaving Puerto Rico. Until, one day, we got in a fight over something silly and I told her that I hated her."

She couldn't hide her shock. "You did? I can't believe you would ever say something like that."

The shame in his eyes was so raw. So wrenching. She looked away, almost embarrassed to have seen it. "Of course I'd never do that now," she heard him say. "But I was an angry guy back then, full of resentment. And that day I finally told her that it was her fault that I'd never be anything more than the manager of a ten-table *taqueria* in San Paolo. I still can't forget the way she winced when I said that. It was like I had slapped her."

"What did she do?"

"She told me I was right."

"Oh, wow."

"Then she told me to leave. She said it was time for me to go live my life. So I did. If it wasn't for her I would've never moved to New York and I probably would've never opened up N.Y. Cuchara. I owe her my dream, Daisy."

The crack in his voice tugged at her heart. Without thinking, she reached out and touched his shoulder. His muscles tightened underneath her fingers, and he cleared his throat. "When I left for New York, I told her that I was going to keep the promise that I had made to her when I was a kid. Eventually, I was able to move her out of our old apartment and into a new house. And I still make sure that her bills are paid and she has whatever she needs, even though she insists that I don't have to take care of her anymore." He took a deep breath before continuing. "That's why she didn't want to come here in the first place. She knows I like my life the way it is— without any ties or responsibilities except for my restaurants. She doesn't want me to ever feel like she's imposing on my freedom or my happiness. Do you understand now why I had to do this? My *mamá* would probably have rather died from cancer than make her son take care of her again. All because I was a stupid kid who said a stupid thing a long time ago."

He looked so ashamed, even though he had nothing to be ashamed of. The need to comfort him overwhelmed any hesitation she had about risking physical contact, so she touched his face. "Don't worry, Brandon. I know what it means to have her here in L.A. I won't back out now. I promise."

He grabbed the hand on his cheek. "I believe you. Thank you."

The unexpected show of affection startled her, and she pulled her hand back quicker than she probably should have. "Listen, I know you've got to get to the restaurant soon, so I can finish these up on my own if you need to leave."

It was more of a statement than a question. Yet he didn't

budge and instead went back to work. She did the same, and they fell into a silent rhythm until only a few things remained in the sink.

"Looks like you need a little more soap," she told him after he handed her a plate.

"Do we have another bottle somewhere? I think I finished this one off."

She smiled at the simple remark. *We.* As though this was her kitchen, too. "There's still some inside there around the edges. Just put in a little bit of water and shake it."

Brandon grabbed the nearly empty plastic bottle from the counter and held it under the open faucet. After filling it about a third of the way, he replaced the squeeze top cap and shook it. But he must've squeezed the middle of the bottle at the same time as he shook it because a spray of bubbles squirted out and landed all over Daisy.

His eyes grew wide and she could tell he was trying hard not to laugh. "I swear that was an accident."

She grabbed the bottle from him and squeezed until bubbles sprayed in his face. "Well, that wasn't."

Brandon wiped his eyes with both hands before taking the bottle back from her and shaking it fast and furious. "So that's what I get for helping, huh?"

"You wouldn't dare," she said as she backed away from him.

He moved toward her, still shaking the bottle. "Oh, but I would."

She stopped when her back hit the door leading to the garage. Holding on to the knob, she braced herself for his payback. But instead of unleashing a spray of soapy suds, Brandon put the bottle down on the counter next to them. "You still have bubbles in your hair," he told her with a smile.

Before she could say or do anything, he reached up and brushed his fingers through the loose strands framing her face. "There," he whispered. "All gone." His smile disappeared along with those unseen bubbles as his hands moved behind her neck and his fingers brushed her jawline.

Her body came alive with the warmth of his touch. She gripped the doorknob and held on as if it were an anchor, something to make sure she didn't drift into dangerous territory yet again.

Then Lorena called for him.

She welcomed the interruption. "Go on. I'll finish these last ones and then head up to bed. I'll see you tomorrow."

"Daisy…"

"Good night, Brandon."

He nodded and headed out of the kitchen. It wasn't until he was gone that she finally exhaled.

· · ·

With his mom finally unpacked and ready for bed, Brandon headed upstairs to take a shower before leaving for the restaurant. It wasn't until he walked into the guest bedroom that he realized he still had most of his things in the closet in the master bedroom—Daisy's bedroom.

He stopped at the closed door and knocked. When she didn't answer, he opened it slowly and called out her name. She still didn't answer, and that's when he saw the light shining from underneath the bathroom door. He walked inside the closet and grabbed another pair of shoes and two more suits. The rest of the stuff could wait until tomorrow.

Then he walked out of the closet and straight into Daisy. "Oh, sorry," he said, dropping his shoes. She jumped backward, as if trying to avoid any additional contact. "I just came in to grab a few things. I didn't get a chance to move my stuff into the other room yet."

She crossed her arms in front of her. She was covered in

a knee-length silk robe, and he had a pretty good idea there was nothing underneath. Her damp hair confirmed that she'd just gotten out of the shower.

"It's okay," she told him. "After all, it's your bedroom. You don't need to explain being in here."

"No, I want to give you your privacy. I'll make sure I tell you ahead of time if I need to come in here. Or," he said with a grin, when she tried to tug down the hem of her robe while keeping the other arm across her chest, "I'll at least wait until you're fully dressed."

"Well, it looks like you got what you need. So…good night then." She lifted her chin, still tugging on her hem.

He draped the suits over the edge of a chair and leaned against the doorframe. *Goddamn* she had nice legs. "Actually, I also needed to talk to you about a couple of things."

Her mouth dropped open. "Right now? Can't it wait until the morning?"

"Unfortunately, it can't. I'm leaving right now for the restaurant so I probably won't see you until tomorrow afternoon."

"Fine. Let me grab my pajamas and you can talk to me through the bathroom door while I change."

She didn't wait for him to answer. Instead, she grabbed a black tank top and a pair of bright pink pants that had been lying on top of the bed then escaped inside the bathroom. He followed and stood in front of the closed door, his hands in his pockets.

"So tell me what you need to tell me," said her slightly muffled voice.

He heard the whisper of fabric falling to the floor and swallowed. Hard. "My mom and Alex want to take you to lunch tomorrow at the restaurant."

The rustle of fabric stopped abruptly. "Tomorrow?"

"Yeah. Alex called a few minutes ago. Is that okay?"

"Um. I guess. Do you think she's going to ask me more questions?"

"Probably. She was on her best behavior tonight so I know she still has a lot she wants to know about you...about us."

"Great," she groaned.

He heard the telltale sound of an elastic waistband snapping into place. He bit his lip to keep in a moan. What he wouldn't give to peel those pink pants right back down her legs.

That was a dangerous train of thought. He cleared his throat and tried to focus. "She already asked me why you aren't wearing an engagement ring."

There was a long pause before she responded, then a quick rustling of fabric. Her tank top, maybe? "Shit. I didn't even think of that."

He nodded and sat down on the bed. "Me either. Who knew we'd need props?"

"So what did you tell her?"

"I told her it was at the jeweler getting resized."

"Ooh, that's a good one."

"But that got me thinking. I can buy you a ring if you want one."

"That's not necessary. This is temporary, remember? Buying a ring would just be a waste of your money."

The door opened and a fully-dressed Daisy stood in the doorway, backlit by the bathroom light, brushing her wet hair. His mouth dropped open. The sight was a thousand times more erotic than what he'd imagined. "Is that what you usually wear to bed?"

"What?" She looked down at herself. "Yoga pants? Yes, I wear them to bed, to the grocery store, to the post office. You might as well get used to them. You've got a thing for suits and I've got a thing for yoga pants."

He was quickly realizing that he had a thing for yoga pants, too. "They look, uh, comfortable."

"Why are you looking at me like that? Were you expecting me to come out in some Victoria's Secret lingerie?" She crossed the room and set a bottle of lotion on the nightstand next to him. "Sorry, but I don't dress to impress when I'm going to bed. And anyways, it's not like I was expecting to put on a show."

That sounded intriguing. "A show, huh? Well, now I have to ask. What kind of show would this be exactly? Would there be singing? Maybe a little dancing?"

She was trying very hard to look annoyed but the smirk on her face didn't convince him. She knew she had walked right into that, and it wouldn't have been normal if he hadn't taken advantage. It was ridiculous how much he enjoyed teasing her.

"Okay, you can stop now," she said and tapped him on his arm with her hairbrush.

"But you haven't given me any details. There are so many things I want to know. Like, for example, what lucky bastard has been on the receiving end of this show? That guy from the wedding?"

"Luis? Please. I could've come to bed wearing a Playboy costume, complete with bunny ears, and he wouldn't have noticed. Just one of the many reasons why we broke up."

The thought of Daisy dressing like a Playboy bunny for another man rammed into him like a truck, and his enjoyment subsided. An uneasiness replaced it, twisting his stomach as if he'd eaten a bad oyster. Since they'd eaten Alex's perfectly cooked chicken, he couldn't blame the queasy feeling on dinner.

You're jealous.

It was a ridiculous idea, given that Brandon hadn't felt jealousy over a girl since the ninth grade. Even more ridiculous that he'd be jealous over Daisy and some imaginary man.

As he watched her apply lotion over her arms and neck, he realized he needed to make an addendum to their original agreement. And it had nothing to do with him being jealous or how delicious her ass looked in those pants and everything to do with keeping up appearances so his *mamá* wouldn't get suspicious.

"So, uh, yeah, there's something else I wanted to talk to you about."

"What's that?" she asked and sat down on the bed next him.

Coconut. She smelled like coconut. His mouth watered. He shook his head and tried to focus. "During our arrangement, I think it would be best if we didn't see other people. You know, it's risky and I don't want that asshole Felipe or anyone else showing up with more pictures, especially now that my mom—"

"I'm fine with that," she said with a shrug.

He'd expected more of a challenge, or an argument about him being too controlling. "You are?"

"Of course. I'm not dating anyone right now anyway."

Good. "Good."

Her eyebrow lifted. "So I'm assuming you're going to be able to stick to this rule as well?"

"Contrary to what you've read in those magazines of yours, I am perfectly capable of being with only one woman. Even if I'm not sleeping with her," he added for both of their benefits. "So we're agreed?"

"We're agreed."

Brandon stood up and headed toward the door. He opened it, but hesitated.

"Was there something else you needed to talk about?" she asked.

"Just so you know…if I was ever lucky enough to see that

show you were talking about earlier, you wouldn't need the Playboy getup. Seeing your ass in those pants again would be enough for me."

He closed the door, happy with the stunned expression on her face.

• • •

It was turning into one of the longest nights of his life. Usually time flew by because the restaurant was so busy, and Brandon loved being in the middle of all the craziness. Whether it was checking in on Alex and her sous chefs in the kitchen or making the rounds out in the dining room, Brandon barely had time to eat, let alone check his watch. But tonight he wasn't feeling it, and instead had retreated into his office to go through paperwork. That only made things worse, though, since he couldn't concentrate on one single damn thing.

What the fuck was wrong with him tonight?

It's because you know she's sleeping in your bed, wearing those pants.

His dick grew hard at the idea of going home early and crawling into bed with Daisy and convincing her to let him take a look at the perfect, rounded ass she'd been hiding from him all this time. To be fair, he knew she had a great body. It was just that she usually didn't wear things so tight or form fitting. But it wasn't just the pants. There was just something hot about seeing her so at home in his home.

Jesus, dude. It's only the first day. How are you going to make it through the next two weeks?

He was saved from answering himself by a knock on his door. Brandon looked up in time to see Christian Santos peek his head inside.

"*Hola, mi amigo.* The food was amazing tonight. I already told Alexa, but I wanted to tell you as well."

Brandon stayed sitting to allow his erection to calm down, but motioned for his friend to come inside. "That's what I like to hear. How about a drink?"

"Sounds good. Everyone else is still finishing dessert, so I have some time."

He took out a bottle of Rémy Martin Louis XIII Cognac and two snifter glasses from his bottom desk drawer. He'd just picked up the high-end liquor on his way to the restaurant. This way he'd always have something nearby to toast on special occasions (like the fake end of his bachelorhood) and for visits from special customers. Christian definitely fell into that category, and he was glad to share the first drink with his friend.

"I'm surprised you're back here in your office tonight. Usually you're out there trying to control everything," Christian teased as Brandon poured two fingers worth into each snifter.

"Believe me, I'd rather be out there than in here, but I was gone most of today so I needed to catch up on some paperwork."

They each held up their glass and gently tapped them against each other before taking a sniff of the refined and complex spirit. It boasted a delicate flowery scent mixed with hints of fig, prune, vanilla, and honey.

"So am I going to see you Saturday?" his friend asked after they'd both taken their first sip.

"Of course," he answered, still savoring the cognac's velvety and rich flavors. "I wouldn't miss it for the world."

"Mira says you're bringing your new fiancée. I had no idea you were even dating someone. Now you're engaged?"

Brandon hadn't planned on talking to Christian about Daisy until the engagement party. The question caught him off guard.

His friend pressed for more information. "So, who is this

woman anyway?"

"Her name is Daisy Robles. She's an event planner who I work with sometimes. And, yeah, we're getting married."

"No shit. For real?"

"For real," he answered without looking at him.

"*Híjole*. I can't believe it. Brandon Montoya is settling down."

He couldn't blame his friend for being so shocked. He never hid the fact that he preferred the single life—not even from the women he dated. He always made it clear that his interest was short-term and nothing they could do or say would change it. There were perhaps two or three who had tried, convincing themselves that they had a real relationship with him. But then he'd explain to them all over again—his restaurants would always be his mistresses and would always come first.

When he'd left his *mamá* in Puerto Rico, he'd promised himself he would be a success. Anything short of that would mean he'd left his family for nothing.

But building a successful empire required working fifteen hours a day, seven days a week, fifty-two weeks a year. Although he had a fantastic manager and head chef back in New York, he still liked to drop in for a few days and check on things. And if the Miami project ever got off the ground then that meant he'd be splitting his time between all three cities. Girlfriends and relationships didn't fit in to that kind of schedule. At least not the ones he'd had.

So he resigned himself to a lifestyle that required no strings and no commitments, all the way down to his leased car and rented condo.

The temporary situation with Daisy merely put a pause on that lifestyle for a couple of weeks. Once it was over, it was back to the single and untangled life for him.

But Christian didn't need to know that.

"What can I say? I finally met the woman for me," he continued, hoping to convince his friend.

"Then I'm happy for you. I really am. I don't even remember my life before Mira came into it. She's changed everything for me. Everything. It's hard to explain, but it sounds like you know exactly what I mean."

He nodded and took another sip. "I do. I really do."

That part was true. Daisy had indeed changed some things in his life.

Starting with his new appreciation of yoga pants.

Chapter Eight

She smelled L.A. Cuchara's menu before even walking through the door. The enticing aroma of garlic and roasted chilies hit her as soon as she exited the car and she took a deep breath. The bundle of nerves ping-ponging inside her gut since she woke up that morning had squelched her appetite. She'd barely slept thanks to obsessing over every possible question Brandon's mother could ask her today during their lunch.

She'd texted Brandon hourly trying to come up with plausible answers to her list of Lorena's potential questions. He'd finally ordered her to go to bed around four in the morning.

Now she'd arrived at the restaurant, running on three hours of sleep and three cups of coffee. Thank God Alexa had stopped by and offered to take Lorena shopping before their lunch. They should already be inside the restaurant, waiting for her to arrive.

Her stomach grumbled as she inhaled a passing waft of garlic and butter. Feasting on L.A. Cuchara's lunch menu would be worth any interrogation by Brandon's mother.

"Fine, you win," she muttered to her angry stomach and then walked into the restaurant.

A pair of breasts met her at the hostess stand. They belonged to the restaurant's manager, Pilar Solis. She knew the woman well. *Too* well.

"Oh, hello, Daisy," she droned and arched one of her pencil-drawn eyebrows. "I didn't think you were meeting Brandon here today. Were you? He's not here right now and I'm not sure when he'll be back."

"Actually, I'm not here for Brandon. I'm here for—"

"Daisy!" Alexa called from a few feet away. As she walked up to them, Daisy smiled at her pretend sister-in-law-to-be. Only a few minutes younger than Brandon, there were certain facial features that made it obvious they were related. But the two could not be more different. Perhaps that was why the restaurant was so successful. While Brandon was a workaholic who got off on marketing reports and financial spreadsheets, Alexa was known for partying with the diners after cooking them a fantastic meal. He drank wine and wore designer suits, Alexa drank beer and shopped for vintage pinup-style dresses. In other words, Alexa was Daisy's kind of people.

"Alexa," Pilar whined, "you didn't tell me that Daisy would be joining your lunch party. But then I should've known that she'd be here with you and your mother. How very sweet." The sarcasm dripped from her Botoxed lips like venom. Then she looked at Daisy. "I apologize but it's still a little strange to think of you as Brandon's fiancée." Was it her imagination or did Pilar's face stiffen when she said the word "fiancée"? Even her perfectly applied makeup could not hide her irritation. She definitely had to text Amara later and let her know that she'd been right all along. Pilar was hot for Brandon. And she didn't just have a resting bitchface. She was a bitch. Period.

"That's okay, Pilar," she said as sweetly as she could muster. "I'm sure you'll get used to it eventually."

"I'm sure I will. It's just that I had no idea you two were even dating. Like no idea, whatsoever. Honestly, I thought he was seeing someone else. In fact, just a few weeks ago he had dinner with this blonde and they looked, um, cozy."

If she'd really been Brandon's fiancée, Pilar's words would've wounded her. Instead, it only antagonized her. "Well, it all happened kind of fast. But then when you know, you know, right? Anyway, we both wanted to keep our personal relationship separate from our business one." And just because she wanted to wipe that ugly smirk off her face once and for all, Daisy added: "Only those closest to us knew what was going on."

The smirk was obliterated. "I see. Well, you certainly hid it very well. Congrats. Enjoy your lunch, you two." Pilar turned her back to them and went back to studying what must've been very important paperwork, leaving Alexa to guide her to the back of the restaurant, into a private room where Brandon's mom was already seated at a table. They were the only three people in the room. There'd be no sneaking out now. Daisy was trapped.

"Lord, help me," she muttered under her breath. But not low enough because as they walked toward their table Alexa asked, "What did you say?"

Daisy thought of a quick save. "I said, 'Lord I'm hungry.' And since you're the head chef here, I'm going to need some recommendations."

"About the food or my mother?"

"Both?"

"Don't worry, you'll do great. Plus, I just broke up with another guy so that should take up most of the lunch conversation."

Alexa winked at her, and for the first time that day, Daisy let her shoulders relax.

"Oh, good! You're here," Lorena said as they took their seats at the table. She reached over and patted Daisy's hand. It was an unexpected gesture that made her tense at first. But the woman's genuine happiness at seeing her eventually made her smile.

"So how was shopping?" she asked her.

Lorena nodded as she unfolded the black linen napkin in front of her. "It was nice. But everything here is so expensive."

"I told you we could've hit some thrift shops, but you insisted we go to the mall instead," Alexa said before tearing into a bread roll.

"*Aye* Alexa, I told you already I don't like to waste my money on old things."

"They're not old, *Mami*. They're vintage."

"Then I guess I'm vintage, too. But that doesn't mean someone should buy me for a dollar."

"No, *Mami*. I'd say you were worth at least nine ninety-nine."

Lorena shrugged and took another piece of bread from the basket. "Eh, but I have the cancer, so I'm probably more like five dollars even?"

Alexa looked at her mom and then they both burst out laughing. Daisy couldn't believe they were joking at a time like this, especially when they were going to meet the oncologist right after lunch. She didn't know what to say, so she pretended to study the menu.

Lorena was the one who noticed she was staying quiet. "It's okay to laugh around me, Daisy."

She looked up and saw them both staring at her. "I know. I was just surprised, I guess."

Alexa nodded in understanding. "Because we joked about her cancer? We know this is serious. Believe me. But if we don't laugh about it, we'll cry, and we're kind of cried out at the moment. Right, *Mami*?"

"*Sí*. No more crying or feeling bad. Instead we laugh, we talk, and we eat. Okay?"

"Okay," Daisy answered.

And for the next hour, they did just that. They chatted about movies and books while feasting on a spicy yet refreshing shrimp *ceviche*; *chile rellenos* stuffed with corn, zucchini, and cheese; and crispy pork belly tacos topped with a pineapple salsa. Each bite was better than the last.

She had to give Brandon and his sister credit. They had outdone themselves with L.A. Cuchara.

"Is anyone up for dessert?" Alexa asked after the waiters cleared their empty plates. "Daisy, your cousin came by earlier and dropped off trays of these amazing-looking caramel-filled donut holes."

"As much as I would love to try those, I don't think I can fit even half of one in my stomach because it's so full. That was such a delicious lunch. Thank you."

"Yes, *mija*. This food was *excelente*."

"Thank you, *Mami*, but I didn't cook it."

"But this is your menu, no? Maybe you don't stuff the *chiles* today or peel the shrimp. But I know this was your food." Lorena reached out and grabbed Alexa's hand. "I know I don't say it all the time, but you make me so proud, *mija*."

Alexa's chin trembled for a second. Then she cleared her throat. "That's the cancer talking."

"This is no joke. I mean it."

The mother and daughter shared a smile, and Daisy could see Alexa was working hard to keep it together. Then the moment passed and the two were back to bickering over whether they should take some *chile rellenos* to Brandon, who had gone to Newport Beach to meet with a distributor.

She was glad for the emotional reprieve. Her own throat had tightened when Lorena told Alexa how proud she was of her. It was obvious that despite her hard and commanding exterior, Alexa had been affected by the words. And Daisy could feel the love between them.

No wonder Brandon had been willing to move heaven and earth to get Lorena to L.A. She didn't just carry the title of mother, she'd earned it and wore it proudly.

For the first time since the whole charade started, Daisy realized the magnitude of what she was doing. What *they* were doing.

She only prayed it wouldn't blow up in their faces.

Chapter Nine

Brandon stared at the degrees displayed on the wall of Dr. Sherman Katz's office, and the massive migraine he'd been fighting all day lessened a bit in pressure and pain. Judging by his credentials, this oncologist was the best of the best. And coupled with what Brandon had heard from various friends and customers, he knew Dr. Katz had the experience and the track record to back up those framed pieces of paper.

"Such a fancy office. I've never been to a doctor's office where they offer you sparkling water," his *mamá* said. "If they have that much money then maybe they have too many patients. We should look for another doctor."

"*Aye, Mami.* We're not looking for another doctor. Besides you already did all of the lab work and tests for this doctor. Do you really want to do it all over again?" he heard his sister ask. She looked over at him with a knowing nod. They'd bet how long it would take before their mother mentioned seeing another doctor. He'd said ten minutes, she'd said five. Guess he was buying everyone dinner later.

Well, everyone except for Daisy. She'd stayed back at

the house even though Lorena had asked her to come. She'd made some excuse about meeting a client but he knew it was because she'd felt uncomfortable. He couldn't blame her. They weren't really her family, and whatever happened next would be something that they had to deal with together—as a family. Daisy had only signed up to be a part of this situation for a few weeks.

The opening door distracted him from thoughts about Daisy, and he stood with everyone else to greet Dr. Katz. After introductions were made, Dr. Katz wasted no time in getting down to business.

"Mrs. Montoya, after reviewing the biopsy results performed by the lab in Puerto Rico, our pathologists agree with the initial findings that you have stage IB cervical cancer."

Although it had been a long shot, there was a small part of Brandon that held out hope the diagnosis had been a complete mistake. His migraine squeezed at his temples so hard he winced. But he pushed aside the pain and tried to focus on what the doctor was saying.

"However, unlike your doctors back home, I'd like to suggest an alternative treatment plan."

"So no chemotherapy?" Brandon asked, his hope fighting to return despite the excruciating ache inside his head.

"Well, not yet, at least. First, I'd like to perform a radical hysterectomy and remove the tumor via robotic surgery. It's less invasive and she can be out of the hospital in two or three days. Then once it's removed, I'd like to start a course of radiation treatments to ensure the cancer has been totally wiped out."

"That sounds good, doesn't it, *Mamá*?"

His mother frowned. "I don't know if I like the idea of a robot operating on me."

"I'd be the one operating on you, Mrs. Montoya," the doctor said with a smile. "Think of the robot as more of an advanced surgery tool, kind of like a high-tech scalpel. Now, I have to tell you, if during the surgery we discover that the tumor is bigger than we thought, then we would have to look at chemo again as a method to shrink it. But I'm pretty confident that won't be necessary."

"What do you say, *Mami*? How about you stay a little longer and have the surgery and the radiation treatments here in Los Angeles?" Alex asked.

"I don't know, *mija*. I do have a life to get back to in Puerto Rico. Maybe I can come back in December and do it then?"

The doctor folded his hands on his desk. "Mrs. Montoya, may I speak frankly? Yes, you are very lucky that your doctor diagnosed your cancer when he did. And although your odds of beating this disease are very high right now, the longer you wait to treat it, the lower your odds become. Women do die from cervical cancer. But you don't have to. I highly recommend you listen to your son and daughter and get your treatment as soon as possible. If not with me, then with someone else."

His mother was wringing her hands in her lap. He knew that meant she was at least considering it. "How long will it take?"

"I can probably schedule you into surgery by the end of the week," Dr. Katz said. "We'll have to wait for your body to heal before you can start the radiation, so that would be at least another four weeks. Then I'd like for you to do twenty radiation treatments. All in all, you're looking at about two months total."

The jackhammering inside his head intensified. Two months? That was a lot longer than two weeks. *Way* longer. Could he convince Daisy to extend their agreement?

"That's a long time, *mijo*. Are you sure Daisy won't mind?" his mother asked. He sat up, startled by her question. Had he said something out loud?

"What are talking about, *Mamá*?" he asked slowly. "Why would she mind?"

"Well, she just moved in, no? That's her home now, too, and I don't want her to think I'm overstaying my welcome."

He breathed a sigh of relief. "Don't be silly. She's going to want you to stay with us for as long as it takes for you to get better."

At least, that's what he was hoping.

. . .

Three hours and four Excedrin later, Brandon came home alone to face Daisy. He and Alex had a sidebar while his mother was in the ladies' room and, like him, his sister was also worried about dragging out the charade longer than originally expected. She'd offered to take their mother back to her house for a few hours so he could have a talk with Daisy.

As he climbed the stairs to the bedroom, he regretted not having Alex with him. Daisy liked Alex and would be less likely to turn her down. Or yell at her.

But as soon as he opened the door, he was glad his sister wasn't anywhere around because what he saw before him gave him an instant hard-on.

Daisy, dressed in only a tank top and an even tighter pair of yoga pants, was bent over a purple mat with her ass pointing toward him. The thought of walking over to her and slamming his groin against those perfect, peach-shaped curves was almost too hard to resist. In fact, he hadn't realized he'd already started walking toward her when she noticed him in the room.

"Oh, hey. You guys are back. How'd it go?" She peered at him through the space between her legs.

"Uh, good, I guess. He came up with a really aggressive

treatment plan and he got my mom to agree to it so..." He shook his head. "I'm sorry, but I really can't focus with you in this position. It's making me want to do some very naughty things to you, and unless you'd like to hear about them or let me do them, it's better if you stand up and face me."

"Sorry," she said with a laugh and then promptly stood right side up and turned to look at him.

Her face was flushed and her chest heaved up and down. Had he known that doing yoga had this affect on women, he would've signed up for a class at his gym a long time ago.

After his afternoon with the oncologist and the stress of his mother's diagnosis, thoughts of yoga and Daisy's fine ass were a welcome reprieve. *Gracias a Dios*, he finally could trust in the hope that his mother would be all right. The treatment would be no picnic, but with the aggressive surgery and radiation, Dr. Katz felt confident she'd make a full recovery. Knowing that lifted an enormous weight off his shoulders. That meant his thoughts could turn to other things.

"You were saying?"

He was saying? Oh, right. He was telling her about his mother's doctor's appointment and how it meant that she'd be staying with him for a little while longer.

"Well, she's agreed to stay in L.A. to have her surgery and the round of radiation treatments. Dr. Katz says she has a very good chance."

"That's wonderful." She threw her arms around his neck to hug him and he wrapped his around her waist to hug her back. "I'm so happy for her, and for you."

They stood there holding each other for a few seconds. He couldn't help but notice how perfect her petite, soft body melded into his taller, harder one. He tried, though, not to think about how the only barrier between him and her bare breasts was a thin piece of stretchy fabric.

Too late. He thought about it and so did another part of

his anatomy. Time to let her go.

"Thank you again, Daisy. I can't tell you enough how much it's meant to me to have you basically put your life on hold in order to help me with my mom's situation."

"You can stop thanking me, Brandon. Seriously. I'm glad to do it. Besides, tomorrow night is Mira and Christian's engagement party and I wouldn't be going if it weren't for you. So I'm grateful to you, too. Besides, I really like Lorena. We had such a great time today during lunch. She's a really good woman. I'd do anything to help her."

If that wasn't an opening he didn't know what was. "Listen. There's something we need to talk about. Why don't you sit down?"

She did what he suggested. "Geez. You're scaring me. I thought you said everything went okay at the doctor's?"

"It did. But, well, you know those radiation treatments I mentioned?"

She looked up at him and nodded. He took a breath and sat down next to her. But, still, he couldn't get the words out. Damn, why was this so difficult? He was a successful entrepreneur who was used to having difficult meetings with business partners all the time. Why was this any different?

Because this business partner is wearing yoga pants to the meeting.

Maybe that was part of it. Or maybe it was just because he was afraid she'd tell him no. Either way, he had to pull off the Band-Aid. "Okay, here's the thing. Turns out the treatments are going to take a lot longer than any of us anticipated."

"How much longer?"

"About two months longer."

"Two months!" She shot off the bed and he followed her as she paced the room.

"I know it's a lot. I know. But if she doesn't stay here and do this now, she's never going to do it. I know my mother.

She'll make excuse after excuse. And the doctor told her this isn't something she can put off. If it's going to happen, it needs to happen now and here in L.A."

She didn't say anything out loud, but he was sure she was talking up a storm in her head.

"How about I give you some time to think about it? You don't have to decide anything right now because I know it's a lot to ask."

When she still didn't answer, he knew there was a real possibility that she could leave at that moment. And he couldn't really blame her. Even he couldn't believe how big of a sacrifice he was asking her to make. And it wasn't like he'd made it any easier on her with his constant sexual innuendos. He headed for the door.

"I'll stay."

She'd said it so soft and low that he could barely make out the words. Once he did, though, he spun around and went to her. "Really? Are you sure?"

"I'm sure. But I want to be clear that I'm not doing it just for you. So don't you dare offer me money or something dumb like that."

"Then why?"

"Because I'd be a terrible person if I walked away when your mom is so close to getting the treatment she needs."

Warmth washed over him. "I wouldn't think you're terrible at all. I'd think you're human. This isn't your fight, Daisy."

"Maybe not. But even though I hate lying to your mother, I know it's for the best. Besides, you're going to need someone here to take care of her after her surgery and between treatments. Both you and Alexa are at the restaurant during the night. What if something happened and no one was around to help her?"

"I could hire someone."

"Wait a second." She put her hands on her hips. "I thought you wanted me stay. Why are you making arguments now about why I shouldn't?"

"Believe me, Daisy—I desperately want you stay. I *need* you to stay. But I also want to be absolutely sure that *you're* sure you want to stay."

"I'm sure."

Overcome with relief, he hugged her tight and lifted her off the ground. She squealed and they both laughed. When he set her down, her face was flushed again and her smile lifted his heart. He couldn't help himself. He had to kiss her. It was brief, but filled with emotion. Especially because she actually kissed him back.

"Thank you," he said when the kiss was over. "Thank you for staying."

"You're welcome. I just hope you don't get sick of having me around."

"I seriously doubt that could ever happen."

In fact, he was more worried about the opposite. What if he liked having her around *too* much? He wasn't sure if his libido could take much more of these friendly hugs and kisses. Sooner or later, every guy reached his limit.

He just wondered what his would be.

Chapter Ten

Daisy watched Mira Alvarez from across the room as she greeted guests with her million-dollar smile. She was the ultimate hostess—warm, inviting, and attentive. But only having spent a total of five minutes talking with her when she and Brandon first arrived at the party, Daisy couldn't tell if Mira was genuine or if she was doing what Daisy was doing—playing a role.

She'd made a real effort to at least look the part of an event planner to the stars. She'd found an online retailer where she could rent a designer cocktail dress without maxing out her credit card. It was a short, black lace and nude sheath dress with a simple off the shoulder neckline. She wore her hair in a messy side bun—a hairstyle she'd practiced doing herself ever since she spotted a photo of an actress wearing it at a red carpet event. Lorena and Alexa had even helped with her makeup and nails before heading to Alexa's house for the night.

She knew she looked good as soon as she spotted the expression on Brandon's face when he first saw her. The desire reflected in his eyes made her catch her breath. It only increased her confidence that she was ready to hold her own with some Hollywood A-listers.

But as soon as they'd driven up to the sprawling Malibu beach house, the little voice in the back of her mind, the one that second-guessed everything she did, roared to life.

Why did she think she could mingle with these people? What in the hell was she smoking when she thought she could just walk up to Mira and, all easy peasy, convince her to hire her as her wedding planner? Even if Mira had once been a regular girl, she sure didn't look like one tonight. She wore her long, dark hair sleek and straight down her back—a stunning contrast against the gorgeous silver gown that hugged her perfect, tanned body.

"Are you going to go over there and talk to her?" Brandon asked. "It's not like you have to take a plane or anything."

She gave him her most evil stink eye. "You're hilarious."

He handed her a glass of champagne. "Here. You look like you could use it."

She sniffed it and shook her head in disgust. "I loathe champagne. And don't you have other people to bother?"

"Not really. Besides, I like bothering you. Especially when I get to rub it in that I was right."

"What do you mean?" she asked and went back to spying on Mira.

"You talk a big game, Daisy, but when it comes down to it, that's all it is. Just talk. Their wedding is out of your league and you know it."

She whipped her head around and glared at him. Anger seethed from every pore in her body as she thought of a few different painful ways she could wipe the smirk off that smug face of his. She hated that she was acting exactly how he thought she'd act—like an amateur who didn't know what the hell she was doing. But she wasn't a goddamn amateur. Daisy grabbed the glass from him, pinched her nose, and downed the drink.

When she started coughing, Brandon took the glass away and laughed. "There you go. Now are you pissed off enough to go over and start talking to the lady?"

"So you were being an ass on purpose?" she asked once she could talk again.

Brandon shrugged. "I figured it couldn't hurt."

Rather than thanking him, Daisy punched him in the shoulder and he nodded that he knew what she'd meant by it. Then she squared her shoulders and walked over to Mira, who was now standing by herself at the bar. She was holding a wineglass but didn't seem too interested in drinking from it.

"Let me guess," Daisy said pointing to the glass. "Right now you're wishing that was a bottle of Corona instead?"

"Heineken," Mira answered with a big smile.

"This is your party. Why don't you just ask for one?"

"Our friends planned this party. This is their home, actually. Guess they didn't think anyone would want beer. Only wine and champagne."

"Did you check their fridge?"

Mira's eyes and smile grew bigger. She set the glass on the bar, grabbed Daisy by the hand, and led her out of the room, down a large a hallway and into an enormous kitchen bustling with servers and trays of food. Within a few seconds, she'd spotted the double door, stainless steel refrigerator and a six-pack of imported beer inside.

Mira grabbed two bottles and asked one of the servers to find her something to open them with.

"It's Daisy, right?" she asked, and Daisy nodded. "Okay Daisy, please remind me to tell Christian that he owes Alberto and Valeria a case of beer."

"A case? Wow, you're being generous. It's not even the beer you wanted."

"You're right. I'll tell him to only buy them a six-pack. Depending on how the rest of the night goes, I may be coming back to finish that one off."

The server returned with a bottle opener and Mira did the honors. Then they knocked their beers together and took a drink.

"This was the best idea," she said after a second gulp. "Thank you, Daisy."

"You're welcome."

They leaned against the counter and watched as the caterers scurried in and out of the kitchen holding different trays of appetizers. Mira stopped the one with the cold shrimp and helped herself to two. Daisy passed but kept an eye out for the guy with the tray carrying ricotta cheese-topped crostini.

"So since we're drinking buddies now, can I confess something to you?"

Daisy turned to face Mira. "Of course," she answered and took another drink

"When I heard Brandon was bringing his fiancée, I imagined she'd be a total bimbo. I'm so glad you're not."

Daisy laughed so hard that beer came out of her nose. Mira found her a napkin and started laughing with her. "Well, I'm glad I'm not either," she said after cleaning off her face.

"I'm sorry. I probably shouldn't have said that out loud. It's just that I've known Brandon now for a while and…"

"And you can't believe he'd ever get married."

"Well, yeah. I'm sorry again. Please ignore me. It's been kind of crazy these past few days—actually, these past few months—and I guess it feels nice to just hang out with someone and drink a beer."

"I get it. One of my favorite things to do is go to my dad's house and kick back and drink a beer or two while we watch a game on T.V."

"Baseball?"

"Soccer."

"Oh, so you're a *futból* fan? *Que bueno*. The L.A. Stars?"

Daisy took a drink and nodded. "I like them, too. But my dad has a satellite so we usually watch the international teams play."

Mira laughed. "What is it about soccer fans and their satellites? My parents have two!"

They spent the next several minutes talking about their favorite teams and sharing stories about playing soccer as kids. While Daisy had only played in elementary school, she was impressed to learn that Mira had also played in college. The more they talked, the more at ease she felt.

Mira was as genuine as they came. She deserved for Daisy to be the same.

After they finished their beers and reapplied their lipsticks, she began. "So now it's my turn to confess something"

"Okay?"

Daisy took a deep breath. "I walked over to you at the bar because I wanted to get to know you so you'd consider hiring me as your wedding planner."

"So asking me about my drink was a sort of a pick-up line?"

"In a way."

"Well, I guess it worked because here we are."

"Look, you seem really cool and nice and actually someone I'd like to be friends with. So I'm not going to do the big selling spiel I had planned, because this is your engagement party and you should be out there enjoying it with people you care about. So thanks for the beer, and I hope that we really can be friends one day even if you don't hire me to be your wedding planner." She turned to leave but stopped. "Oh, and one more thing. Please don't tell Brandon about how bad I messed this up, okay? Thanks."

She could've kicked herself.

Why on earth did she think she could pretend to be this confident, big shot wedding planner when she couldn't even share a beer with someone like Mira?

Daisy slinked back to the main party room and looked around for Brandon. She eventually found him talking to three men near the bar. He fit into this crowd with his perfect suit and perfect hair and perfect smile. No wonder he had balked at first at introducing her to Christian. She didn't belong in his world. And she'd just ruined the only reason why she'd agreed to be a part of it in the first place.

"So what do you think of instead of a champagne fountain, we have a beer fountain at the reception?"

Daisy turned around and found Mira standing behind her holding two more bottles of beer. "Well, I'd say, first of all, nobody does champagne fountains anymore anyway, so why not? And second of all, I'd say it's your damn wedding so you should be able to do whatever the hell you want."

Mira handed her a bottle. "I think you're pretty cool, too. And I think I need someone like you on my side to help me get through all this wedding stuff."

"Confession time again. I've never planned a celebrity wedding before."

"Well, I've never been in a celebrity wedding before."

"You're sure you don't want someone more… Hollywood?"

"Why? So they can listen to all my ideas and then go ahead and do the exact opposite?"

"As long as you're sure?"

"I'm sure," Mira said and tapped Daisy's bottle with hers before taking a drink.

A good-looking man came up behind Mira and stole her bottle. "Where'd you find the beer?"

Mira took it back from him. "Daisy and I stole it from the Alonsos' refrigerator."

The man looked at Daisy with raised eyebrows. "Well, could Daisy steal one for me, too?"

She tried to look serious but was probably failing. "It depends."

"On what exactly?" the man asked with an amused grin.

"On whether Mira here wants another one. The bride always comes first."

Mira laughed and patted the man on the shoulder. "Too bad, Esteban. Guess you'll just have to drive to the nearest liquor store and get your own."

"Wow, little sister. I never imagined you'd turn into one of those bridezillas."

"Surprise. Anyway, as much as I would love to continue our conversation, Daisy, I guess I better make some more rounds. Let's exchange numbers before you leave, okay?"

Mira handed Esteban her bottle and walked away. "It sounds like you and my sister are going to be friends?" he asked before taking a drink.

She shrugged. "I hope so."

Perhaps it was the second beer, but Daisy felt downright giddy. The night had gone so much better than she had expected. And at that moment, all she could think about was going to Brandon and telling him all about it.

Huh. That's new.

Since when did she go running to tell Brandon anything? It was true that he had played a part in getting her to this moment. But a few weeks ago, she probably would've thanked him via email rather than in person. Now, she actually *liked* talking with him. Hell, she had even started to tolerate his teasing. She was getting used to Brandon. And every day they were together, the bumblebees calmed a little more.

The goose bumps, however, were still as strong as ever.

· · ·

Fuck, he wanted to walk over and touch her. It didn't matter if it was her arm or waist or that luscious ass of hers. He wanted to show that jerk-off that she belonged to him.

He'd been watching Daisy for a while now. He'd heard her laugh across the room and noticed her talking with Mira and some man. Then Mira left and Daisy and the man stayed in the corner, still talking and drinking from beer bottles. He'd been wondering how it had gone with Mira ever since she'd downed that glass of champagne he gave her. They'd both disappeared for a while and he assumed they were hitting it off. He'd wanted her to spend time and be friendly with Mira. What he didn't want was to watch her be friendly with a man who wasn't him.

Brandon set his drink on the bar and interrupted his friends' conversation about their recent vacation. "Excuse me, but I think I've neglected my beautiful fiancée long enough. I'm going to go find her."

Determined to remind Daisy why they were there in the first place, he weaved in and out of the small crowd, narrowing in on the small looking man and the fact that she was laughing again and touching his arm. How dare she flirt with some stranger after making such a big deal about him being the one who might get caught with someone else? She wouldn't even be at this party if it weren't for him, and it needled him that she was using it to pick up her next boyfriend rather than her next client.

Something came over him at that moment, and he had to fight the urge to pick her up and throw her over his shoulder and carry her out of this house. Luckily, some sense of rationality nudged its way into his caveman brain, and he caught himself before he reached them.

"There you are, *mi amor*. I've been looking all over for you."

Daisy turned to look at him. "You have?"

"Of course. You know I can't go that long without having you by my side." He looked at the small man, who now didn't look so small up close, and offered his hand. "I'm Brandon Montoya, Daisy's fiancé."

The man's surprised expression told Brandon that his instincts were right. This man believed Daisy was available. That unfamiliar feeling twisted at him again, and this time he couldn't help but put his other arm around her waist and pull her toward him.

"Good to meet you, Brandon. I'm Esteban Alvarez, Mira's brother."

His irritation grew deeper. He felt Daisy unhook herself from his grasp, but before she could totally extricate herself, he grabbed her hand. "Ah, Mira's brother. I think I've heard her mention you before. You're the music teacher with a wife and twins on the way. Is she here, too?"

She squeezed his hand then. Hard. But he didn't care if she was angry—she needed to know what kind of guy she'd been flirting with.

"Actually, that's our other brother. I'm an oncologist at USC and as single as they come."

"Esteban works in the same office as Dr. Katz, and I was just telling him how grateful we all are that he's your mother's doctor," Daisy explained.

A twinge of guilt poked at him and Brandon let her go. "Yes, of course we are very grateful."

"Well, I hope everything works out and Dr. Katz can give her the help she needs. Now, if you'll excuse me, it looks like they're getting ready to do some toasts so I better find the rest of my family."

After the doctor walked away, Daisy grabbed Brandon's hand again and pulled him into the corner of the room. "What the hell was that all about? You were kind of a jerk to him."

Irritation flashed again. "No, I wasn't. It's not my fault I thought he was the other brother."

"Not that. I'm talking about the way you interrupted our very nice conversation just so you could make it very clear that we were engaged."

"Well, I thought that was the point of us being here tonight—to let people know we're a couple. And maybe I wouldn't have had to say anything if you had already told him you had a fiancé."

"We just met, for Pete's sake. What was I supposed to do? Introduce myself and add the word 'engaged' after my name like some damn credential?"

The wild look in her eyes told him she was angry. It should've made him retreat—save the battle for another time and place. But he didn't. Couldn't. They'd made an agreement to act like a couple in front of others, and yet she'd barely spoken to him since they'd arrived. Was he supposed to stand around like an ass while she flirted with a total stranger? Okay, maybe she wasn't exactly flirting, but it still wasn't right. He was done being ignored.

"Yes. That's exactly what you're supposed to do. I don't care if he's a doctor or the guy who makes your sandwich at Subway. Pretend or not, for the next couple of months, *tu eres mia*, and I'm not planning on sharing you with anybody."

If she wanted to argue about him saying she belonged to him, she couldn't, because at that moment people started clinking their glasses. He turned away from her and saw Christian and Mira walking to the center of the room. His friend was handed a wireless microphone, and he waved his hand in the air so everyone would turn their attention to him.

"Before it gets any later and some of you get any drunker, we wanted to take a moment to say thank you for being here tonight to celebrate our engagement," Christian announced. "Servers are going around the room offering glasses of champagne, so if you don't have one already in your hand, please take one."

Brandon grabbed two glasses from the server as he passed and offered one to Daisy. He thought she'd refuse since she supposedly hated champagne and was obviously still mad, but she placed her bottle on the tray and took the glass. Once it seemed as if all of the champagne flutes had been distributed, Mira's brother joined the couple in the middle of the room.

"Now, everyone, please raise your glass and toast to Christian and Mira," Esteban said. "Congratulations you two!"

The room filled with the sound of glasses clinking, shouts and whistles, and a growing chant of "*Beso. Beso. Beso.*" Christian nodded and took Mira in his arms and gave her the kiss that everyone wanted to see, complete with a dramatic dip at the end. Their audience hooted and hollered in approval and then clapped when they finally came up for air. When the noise settled down, Christian spoke again.

"I was telling someone the other day that love changes things. It changes how you see the world and even how you see yourself. If you had told me six months ago that I'd be getting engaged to the love of my life, I would've laughed in your face. I know now that I only thought that way because I didn't believe there was someone out there who could love me for me, with all my faults and issues. But it turns out there was and once I found her, I knew I could never let her go. And now I want everyone to be as happy as we are. That's what love does to you, I guess. That's why I want to take this opportunity to congratulate one of my friends who has also recently found love. Brandon, please come up here and bring that beautiful fiancée of yours with you."

Brandon froze. Did Christian really just call him out? He turned to Daisy and could see she was just as shocked as he was. Grabbing her hand, he pulled her with him to the center of the room and they were greeted with warm hugs from both

Christian and Mira.

The crowd started chanting again. "*Beso. Beso. Beso.*"

It was rude to ignore them, wasn't it? Brandon turned to Daisy, whose eyes grew wider as he approached. He expected to see fear in them. Instead, he saw desire. It was the way she had looked at him that night of the wedding. And that's when he knew what he'd been craving all this time. He put his hands on her face and gently lifted her head as he lowered his. He kept his eyes open until the moment their lips touched, fitting perfectly against each other. They started slow and soft as if they were unsure of what they were doing. But desire like theirs never forgets. Never forgives. And so the kiss turned hard, almost punishing. Her mouth eventually opened, perhaps to steal some oxygen, and he took the opportunity to thrust his tongue inside. He could still taste the sweetness of the champagne mixed with the bitterness of the beer, and it made him drunk with need. If he could, he'd kiss her like this all night.

Instead, he felt a tap on his shoulder and heard the sounds of people hooting and whistling loudly. "Good thing this wasn't a kissing contest, right, Mira?" he heard Christian mumble behind him.

It took everything he had to tear his lips from Daisy's and drop his hands from her face. She must've been leaning on him because once he let go, she stumbled forward, and he reached out to steady her with one arm around her waist.

After Christian made another joke to the crowd, Brandon lowered his head and whispered into her ear, "Now every man in the room knows that you belong to me. And for the record, I'm tired of pretending that I don't want you in my bed. So just say the word and we'll go home so I can fuck you the way I've been wanting to fuck you since you walked down my stairs in this dress."

Not ready to see her reaction to his proposition, Brandon

walked away from Daisy to join the crowd of well-wishers who were now surrounding Christian and Mira. As he waited his turn, the enormity of what he'd just said and done began to weigh on him.

Although he'd intended the kiss to be a statement to those watching, it turned out to be more of an exclamation point on his own pent up frustration. He knew he'd lost control with his mouth and his words. Still, he wasn't going to apologize for telling her the truth. Wasn't that what she said she had wanted? He was a grown-ass man and shouldn't have to hide his desires—especially from the woman pretending to be in love with him. It all seemed so silly. But the ball was in her court now. If she wanted him, then she'd have to be the one to make the next move. He just hoped that move didn't involve leaving his house and canceling their agreement.

He felt someone tug on his sleeve and the night took a turn he'd never seen coming.

"Take me home."

The words were breathed, rather than spoken. Yet he'd heard them loud and clear. He spun around and found Daisy staring at him with an expression on her face he couldn't quite figure out. "What are you saying?"

She grabbed his hand and pulled him toward her. "I'm saying take me home. And take me to bed."

• • •

They didn't speak once they said their good-byes, or in the car, perhaps afraid one of them would say something to stop this. To his credit, Brandon drove only about fifteen miles over the speed limit.

It was still too slow as far as Daisy was concerned.

She couldn't explain it. Even now as Brandon zoomed down the freeway she couldn't have said what it was that made her decide to finally sleep with him tonight.

After all, she should've been offended that he was obnoxious enough to think she belonged to him, or that he could brand her with a kiss in front of all those people. But rather than consumed with anger, she was enflamed with lust. Maybe it was the high of everything that happened with Mira. Or maybe it was the realization that in a party filled with so many beautiful, famous women, she was the one Brandon wanted to take home.

Or maybe, like him, she was just tired of pretending.

As he pulled into the driveway, she silently thanked God that Lorena was staying the night with Alexa. Whatever was about to happen between them, she didn't need to worry that his mother would be around to hear it.

Brandon parked and got out of the car. He made his way to her side and opened the door. He offered his hand and she took it. The contact made her inhale sharply. But then he let go and motioned for her to head to the house. She walked carefully up the brick pathway, stopping when she reached the front door. Brandon inserted the key and pushed the door open, again motioning for her to go ahead of him.

While she hadn't expected him to jump on her in the driveway, his continuing silence and physical distance made her wonder if he'd changed his mind. She stopped in the middle of the foyer after hearing the door close behind her. "So we should talk about what—"

He grabbed her left wrist and spun her around to face him. Then he grabbed her other wrist, making her drop her small clutch purse on the floor, and walked her backward until she was up against the front door, pinning her hands on each side of her head. "I think we're done talking."

He claimed her mouth in one long, brutal kiss, finally giving her the physical contact she'd been waiting for. She surrendered to him and their tongues dueled in a desperate dance to taste each other, feed on each other. Brandon moved his lips to her neck while his hands still pinned hers. "God, I've thought about touching you like this for so long. So damn long."

So had she. It wasn't until he kissed her at the party that she'd realized just how long she'd been waiting. She was a starved woman who'd been tricking herself into thinking she wasn't that hungry. His kiss blasted through any remnants of self-control, and she was ready to finally indulge in her cravings.

"I want you, Brandon," she confessed.

He lifted his head to look at her. "And I want you, Daisy. *Necesito.* You know that. I'm ready to take you, but I need to know for sure. I need to know you're ready for this. Because if you're not, I'll let you go right now."

The thought of Brandon not touching her again was inconceivable. She met his darkened eyes. "I'm sure. Make me yours, once and for all."

It was the permission he needed. He let go of her wrists and encircled her with his arms. She threw hers around his neck and pulled him down for another consuming kiss. He groaned and it thrilled her to know that she had caused him to do that. Their passion became a hurricane of heated energy, and she was swept up in its vortex, hurtling toward a place of raw sexual need that she'd never experienced before. If this is what it meant to become lost in another person, then she didn't want to ever be found.

"I'm going to go crazy if I don't touch you, Daisy. *Dejame tocarte.*"

"Yes…touch me, please."

Brandon dropped to his knees and lifted the hem of her cocktail dress, pushing it up around her waist. "Careful," she whispered. "The dress is rented. I have to send it back tomorrow."

He hooked a finger under the waistband of her black thong. "Is this rented, too?"

"No. Why?"

In one swift move, he ripped the flimsy material off her body and spread her lips open. The warmth and wetness of his tongue buckled her knees as he licked her with one long stroke, and she cried out. Her belly tightened and twisted with so much pleasure that she involuntarily arched her hips against him, her body begging on its own for more than just his tongue. He responded by tapping his fingers against her swollen mound. The light, teasing pressure drove her insane and she found herself gyrating against his hand.

"You like that, don't you? Well, you're going to like this even more," he said, and slid a finger inside her. They both gasped. "Fuck, you're so hot and wet already." He continued to pump his finger in and out of her while his mouth went back to sucking on her clit.

Small tremors of pleasure vibrated from her core and fanned out to every nerve in her body. She hovered at the edge, not ready to let go just yet. The longer she held in the explosion, the bigger the final bang would be. But her willpower was no match for Brandon's expert tongue and before she knew it, the rumbling of a full-blown orgasm made her legs begin to quake. "I'm going to come. Oh my God, I'm going to come so hard," she said between long, deep breaths.

And then it happened. Full-on detonation.

Did that scream come from her? It must have. Through her blissful, glorious haze of sweet satisfaction, she watched as Brandon reached to pick up her purse. Then he took her in his arms and lifted her up. "What are you doing?" she mumbled.

"Taking you to my bed, so I can finally drive my cock deep inside you like we both need me to do."

Before, she would've protested and made some remark about breaking his back or insist she didn't need to be carried.

But because she still didn't trust the steadiness of her legs, and because she couldn't think of a valid argument why he shouldn't, she laid her head against his arm and allowed him to hold her. On the way up the stairs, the only sounds he made were deep breaths that fanned her hair. He didn't kick open the bedroom door like in some cheesy romance movie. Instead he nudged it open with his shoulder, tossed her purse to the side, and then gently put her down in front of him when they reached the bed. There, the gentleness stopped. Brandon dropped his head and kissed her hard. Their mouths opened so their tongues could find each other again. But it wasn't enough.

Daisy reached between their bodies and pressed against the thick bulge between Brandon's legs. "Do you feel that, Daisy?" he asked against her mouth. "My cock is so hard because of you. It wants to be inside you so fucking bad."

His words turned her internal temperature to scorching. Her sex clenched at the thought of finally being filled by Brandon. "I want it inside me, too," she whispered and started pulling his shirt up and then unbuckling his belt. They broke apart so he could take the rest of his clothes off. She sat down on the bed and watched as the full picture of Brandon's beautiful naked body came together. His engorged penis jutted out from his body, and Daisy licked her lips at the sight of its glistening head.

Brandon knew exactly what she was thinking. "*Cariño*, as much as I want to feel those lips around my dick, I don't think I could handle it. Stand up and turn around."

Disappointment at not being able to taste him subsided as soon as she felt his hands on her shoulders and his warm lips nibbling her ear. She sighed and arched her neck to give him better access.

After licking and tasting her neck, he pulled the zipper of her dress down and brushed it off her shoulders, letting it fall to the ground. His lips moved to her bare back, and she shivered—not from the cold, but from the trail of heat he made with his mouth. Brandon unhooked her bra and then covered her breasts with his palms. She fell against him, and he moaned as her bare ass made contact with his erection.

From behind, he wrapped his arms around her and said into her ear, "God, I can't believe I finally get to hold you like this. Your body feels so good against mine."

She nodded and closed her eyes, caught up in the sensation of their naked bodies rubbing against each other. His hard arms felt amazing against her soft skin. Their position was so intimate, so sensual. Heat rushed to her face, and she was sure she was blushing. Before Amara's wedding, she would've never imagined being this close to Brandon. Sure, the thought of him in bed had crossed her mind a few times. How could it not? But this was different. This was unimaginable. Unthinkable.

Because if she did let herself think about it much longer, she might have just run out of the room.

Perhaps sensing a change in her passion, Brandon made sure Daisy came back to him by moving one hand between her legs. Her eyes opened as a finger circled her clit and then penetrated her folds. "That's what I thought," he said as his lips brushed her shoulder. "Your pussy is still dripping with desire for me."

He whipped her around then and pushed her softly onto the bed so he could take off her heels. Now they were both completely naked. He knelt between her legs and proceeded to feast like a starved man on her breasts as he guided her up toward the head of the bed. She gasped as he alternated between sucking her nipples into thick, stiff peaks and teasing them with slow, light licks. She couldn't take much more.

"Please, Brandon," she begged for what he'd promised her.

"Almost, *mi amante*. Almost." He reached beyond her to the single drawer of the small nightstand table and brought back a square foil packet. She watched through half-closed eyelids as he tore it open with his teeth and then rolled the condom onto his penis. Then he grabbed one of the new sham-covered pillows she'd bought and maneuvered it underneath her ass. "This will make sure that you can take me as deep as possible. Are you ready, Daisy?"

She wasn't. But that didn't matter. All that mattered was feeling Brandon inside her.

So she nodded.

He spread her thighs open with his hands, taking the time to kiss the inside of each one. With one hand he guided himself slowly to the entrance of her sex and then pushed inside. A grunt escaped his lips, while she inhaled a quick, deep breath. He didn't move for a couple of seconds. "*Aye*, you feel so good," he told her. "I wanted to take my time, savor this. But feeling your tight pussy…I don't think I can wait much longer. I need to fuck you. "

Being filled by him was much more than she had expected. Her body was humming with electricity, every nerve vibrating with lust. She couldn't come again, could she? She'd never had an orgasm during intercourse before. Her hardened nipples and pulsing core told her that was all about to change.

"Then do it, Brandon. Dear God, do it now."

He withdrew from her and she whimpered. Actually whimpered. But then with one quick thrust, he impaled her once again. Daisy closed her eyes as her orgasm overtook her.

"Look at me when I'm inside you. I want to see you come," he ordered.

She forced her eyes open and they locked gazes just as the last wave of pleasure rolled through her body. Neither looked away as he continued to drive into her over and over again. His breathing became as labored as hers, and the veins along his neck strained with tension. She wanted to give him the release he so desperately needed and the pleasure he'd already given her twice.

Daisy reached up and dug her nails into his forearms. "Harder," she urged. "Make me yours."

He hooked his arms around her legs and slammed into her with two quick thrusts. His face turned red as his body jerked and shuddered. "Fuuuuuck," he yelled and collapsed on top of her.

She lay still for a few seconds, waiting for her pulse and heart rate to slow down.

"Wow," he murmured into her neck after they both finally caught their breath.

"This is so not how I thought tonight would end," she said with a laugh.

He raised his head to look at her. "Me either. Okay, maybe I did think it a little. That dress was hot."

She laughed again and pushed him off her. He gave her another long kiss. "Damn, I really don't want to go to the restaurant tonight. Maybe I should just stay here in bed with you?"

Did he really want to stay? Or was he just saying it so she could be the one to tell him to go? "Do what you want."

He raised his eyebrow at her comment. "What's that supposed to mean?"

"It means what you think it means. I'm telling you to do what you want. Go to the restaurant or stay here."

The raised eyebrow didn't go down. "Okay, then I'm going to jump in the shower and get dressed and head over to the restaurant for an hour to check on supplies for tomorrow's brunch service. But then I'm coming straight back to this bed, so don't you dare put any clothes on."

He gave her a quick kiss and escaped to the bathroom before she could respond. Being alone gave her some precious time to absorb what had just happened—until she heard a muffled ringing coming from the end of the bed. Covering herself with the robe she kept on a nearby armchair, Daisy went searching for her ringing purse. But when she pulled out her phone and recognized the number, she'd wished she'd never found it.

Just answer it and get it over with.

Daisy pushed the button and said, "Hello, Mom."

"Why is it that I'm the last to know that you're engaged to the famous restaurant chef Brandon Montoya?"

"I'm fine, Mom. Thanks for asking. And he's not the chef, he owns the restaurant."

"Stop the sarcasm. So is this true? Are you really engaged? My friend Gloria sent me a picture of you two at Christian Santos' engagement party. It was on some website."

Damn, those paparazzi worked fast. "Yes, I'm engaged. There, I've confirmed the rumor. Anything else?"

"Anything else? Are you kidding me? I want details. How long have you two been dating? Are you living together? When's the wedding?"

"Mom, it's late and I was actually already in bed. Can we talk about this later?"

"I guess. How about we do brunch tomorrow? Then you can catch me up on all of the details and we can start planning the wedding. Oh, I just had the best idea. I'm going to throw you and Brandon an engagement party at the club. Tomorrow I can show you the ballroom and we can look at menus—"

"Mom, stop. I'm not ready to start planning anything yet. And I can't do brunch tomorrow anyway. Some other time, okay?"

"Fine. Just as long as we talk. I'm sorry for getting so carried away, it's just so very exciting. I can't believe you're going to marry somebody so rich and famous. It's what I always wanted for you, you know that, don't you?"

"What about love, Mom? Aren't you happy that I'm marrying someone who loves me and who I love back?" It didn't matter that it wasn't true now because when she became engaged for real then it would be.

"Well, of course, dear. It's just that love doesn't pay the bills."

And there they were. The words she'd heard most of her life. Her mother used them to justify leaving her dad. Yet she never once had a convincing argument as to why she left Daisy, too.

She promised to call in a few days and then rushed her mother off the phone before she could say anything more to infuriate her. Daisy pressed her cool palms against her burning cheeks. She'd become as heated as when she'd first answered the call but for all kinds of different reasons. Maybe one day she'd have a real relationship with her mother. But that day would not be today or tomorrow or even next week. How could she, when her mother proved time and time again that she'd never change? She'd always be more concerned with appearances and material things than family.

And after trying to convince her mother that this fake engagement was based on love, it just seemed all that more clear to her that it wasn't. There was no denying that they were attracted to each other. But now that they'd scratched their proverbial itch, things could calm down.

And Brandon would forget that he ever wanted her in the first place.

Still, she had to keep her distance for her own sake. Especially now that she'd landed the Santos-Alvarez wedding. She needed to show Brandon that what happened tonight didn't have to change anything. It couldn't.

Then Brandon walked out of the bathroom in nothing but a towel around his waist.

Daisy tugged tighter at her robe and ignored the instant

rush of heat between her legs. "Um, aren't you going to get dressed?"

"My clothes are in the other room, remember? But not for long. I'll move them back tomorrow."

"Oh, you're going to start sleeping in here?" The thought really hadn't occurred to her.

He moved to the side of the bed and picked up his discarded suit and other items. "Judging by your tone, I guess I'm not."

"No, it's fine. I just thought…"

"You thought what? This was a one time thing?"

"Well, yeah. We agreed—"

"We did agree to keep this arrangement platonic but that was before. Now that I know how amazing it feels to be inside you, I'm not sure if I can *not* be inside you again."

"I'm just confused, Brandon. I need time to think about things."

"Fine. I'll leave you alone tonight. But sooner or later, we're going to have to decide whether this door stays open or whether it's going to be locked for good," he said, and walked out of the room.

For a while, Daisy sat on the bed, wondering whether she'd be able to go back, to return to the way it was *before*. Like Brandon said, now that she'd had him it was going to be harder to not have him again.

When sleep couldn't be denied any longer, she took a quick shower, dressed, and got back into bed. She heard him come home a few hours later. And when she realized he'd gone back to the other bedroom to sleep, relief, and a tiny bit of disappointment, washed over her.

Chapter Eleven

"I knew it!"

Daisy pulled her cell phone away from her ear before another one of her cousin's outbursts rendered her deaf. She should've expected such a high-pitched reaction to her confession that she'd slept with Brandon. "All right, all right, Angela Lansbury. Calm down."

"I totally knew you two wouldn't be able to keep your hands off each other living under the same roof. Didn't I tell you? Didn't I?"

"Yes, Amara. You told me," she said and sighed.

"So how was it?" her cousin whispered into the phone.

"How do you think it was?"

"Daisy…"

"Amara…"

"Fine. Don't tell me. So are you going to do it again?"

That was the million dollar question. Wasn't it? He'd left early the next morning for New York. They'd only exchanged text messages over the past three days, and their conversations were always about Lorena.

"I don't know," she told Amara. She heard an exasperated sigh on the other end of the phone. "What's that for?"

"You know I'm just worried about this whole situation. I'm afraid—"

"You're afraid I'm going to get hurt, I know. But we already talked about this. I'm not some silly groupie who's going to think there's more to this than there is."

"Yes, but now that the relationship has become physical, it may be harder to keep your emotions separate. Like I said, I just don't want you to get hurt."

Neither did she. Perhaps Amara had a point. "I guess I need to talk to Brandon when he gets back tomorrow night," she said as she leaned on the kitchen's center island. "Maybe we do need some boundaries."

"I think that would be best. Oh, hey! I almost forgot to tell you. You're famous again."

Daisy stood back up. "What do you mean?"

"There was an article online about you and Brandon getting engaged. Nice photo, by the way."

"Oh, that. Thanks. We decided the only way for that bastard Felipe not to profit from our fake engagement was to send out a press release and photo to all kinds of media outlets. We figured no one would want to pay him money for a crappy photo of an engaged couple making out. Sounds like it worked."

"Good. Hopefully it means that creep will stay away from you guys from now on."

"Yep. Now I guess I just have to figure out how to get Brandon to stay away," she said drily.

"Ha ha," her cousin replied. "Seriously, though. You know I nag because I love you, right?"

"I know. I love you, too. I'll let you go since you have to get up at the ass crack of dawn. Those rolls won't bake themselves, you know."

"You're full of jokes, aren't you? Okay, good night. Call me tomorrow."

They said another round of good-byes before Daisy finally put her phone down. She looked around to make sure she'd put away everything from dinner. Deciding the kitchen was clean, she picked her phone back up, turned off the light, and headed toward the stairs. The sound of keys jangling and the lock on the front door jiggling made her stop dead in her tracks.

It was after nine at night, which meant Alexa would be smack dab in the middle of dinner service, so it couldn't be her getting ready to come through the door. Within a span of a few seconds, Daisy imagined about fifteen scenarios that involved her leaving her keys in the door and some serial killer finding them for her.

So when the door opened and Brandon walked inside, she let out a long, relieved breath.

"What are you doing here?" she asked in a loud whisper so she didn't wake Lorena.

"I live here, remember?" he responded as he closed the door again and locked it.

"I meant what are you doing here tonight? You weren't supposed to be back until tomorrow."

He shrugged. "My meetings finished early, and I wanted to make sure I was around to spend some time with my mom before her surgery."

"Oh. Well, you should've called or texted. I was about to karate chop your ass."

"Really? Because judging by the look on your face when I walked in, it looked like you were going to pee in your pants instead."

"Funny. Well, welcome home. Good night."

"Actually, there was another reason why I couldn't wait to come home," he said and reached into his messenger bag. "I bought you something while I was in New York."

Daisy froze as she recognized the distinctive robin's egg blue-colored bag he was holding as he walked toward her. She swallowed hard as he pulled out a small black velvet box from the Tiffany & Co. shopping bag. Then he handed it to her. "Go ahead. Open it."

How could she open it if she couldn't even raise her arms to take it from him? Helpless, she could only ask, "Is it a ring?"

He laughed. "What gave it away? Well, take a look, silly. It's just a ring. It won't bite you."

Maybe not. Didn't mean she still wasn't afraid of it for some unreasonable reason.

Her brain eventually connected to her body, and she took the velvet box from Brandon and opened it.

It wasn't just a ring. It was the queen of all rings. And queen, as in queen of heart-shaped diamond rings. She had no idea what carat size it was, but she did know that it wasn't itty bitty. In fact, it was biggie biggie.

"Wow, Brandon. It's…it's. It's… Wow. This must've cost you a lot."

"Don't worry about that. Go ahead and try it on."

She nodded and tried to smile as big as she could as she slipped it on her finger. It fit her a little loose. Did she imagine its heaviness on her hand? Okay, now she really was being silly. It was a piece of jewelry. Nothing more, nothing less.

"So what do you think?"

She thought it was too much. "It's beautiful, Brandon. But I think it's too much. Besides, I thought we agreed I didn't need a ring."

"I know we did, but that was when we thought we'd only be fake-engaged for two weeks. Now that it's going to be a lot longer than that, I figured this would stop people's questions."

"Well, you didn't have to spend so much…"

"I know, but I figured since you won't let me give you any

money, afterward you could sell it or exchange it."

His matter-of-factness stung. The ring, like Daisy, was replaceable. It didn't matter to him if they slept together again or not. When this fake engagement was over, he'd just find someone else to take her spot in his bed.

I told you so. You're nothing to him. He would've asked any woman to pretend to be his fiancée. You just happened to be the one to say yes.

Anger swelled inside her. But not at him. He'd never promised her anything except mind-blowing sex. This was all on her.

"Good night, Brandon," she said and left him standing in the foyer.

She was halfway up the stairs when she heard him behind her. "Good night? That's all you've got to say to me?"

"What do you want me to say?"

"I don't know? How about telling me why you're so pissed off, for starters."

They'd reached the bedroom, and Daisy finally turned around to face him. "I'm fine and I already told you the ring is fine."

"Fine? Really? I'm no expert, but I know that a ring like that can be described in at least a hundred different words and 'fine' is definitely not one of them."

"What do you want me to say? Yes, it's a beautiful, expensive ring but…"

"But what? I don't understand. The salesman at Tiffany's said any woman would love to get this ring. Pilar even agreed."

She threw up her hands. "Pilar? You took Pilar to Tiffany's to pick out a ring for me?"

"Yes. I needed a woman's opinion."

"What guy takes another woman to pick out his fiancée's ring?"

"But you're not even really my fiancée."

"*I* know that, but she doesn't. Now she's going to be suspicious. She already thinks she should be the one you're engaged to…for real!"

"Wait. Are you jealous?" he asked, more amused than she appreciated.

She put her hands on her hips, prepared to defend herself against such a ridiculous accusation. "What? Of course not. It's just that—"

"It's just that what?"

"It isn't me!" she yelled, forgetting that Lorena was still asleep downstairs.

Brandon looked even more confused. "The ring?"

"Yes, the ring. It's extravagant, Brandon. It's showy. It's everything I'm not. You didn't buy this ring for me. You bought it for the woman who's pretending to be your fiancée. So let's be honest here. I'm merely a prop in your charade… just like this stupid ring. Except I'm also good for fucking once in awhile."

"Wait a second," he said and stepped closer to her. "I don't think of you like that, Daisy. You have to believe me."

"Why should I believe anything you say? You're an OCC."

"A what? Never mind. You should believe me because it's true. We have a connection. I feel it and I know you feel it, too. And it's getting stronger. That's why I had to stop pretending the other night that I didn't want you as badly as I did. As I do. Having sex with you was more than I ever could have dreamed of, and I'm not saying that just because I want to have sex with you again. You're not some prop I'm going to throw away when this is all over. You mean something to me, Daisy."

His words dug in and grabbed hold of her heart. "You don't have to lie to me, Brandon."

He sighed with such exasperation, she knew he was becoming frustrated. "I'll prove it to you. If you didn't mean anything to me would I know that you like strawberry jam on your pancakes instead of syrup? Would I know that you prefer to drink Diet Pepsi, but if a place only serves Diet Coke then you prefer iced tea? Would I know that you got that little scar on your knee from when you fell down rollerblading for the first time?"

"Impressive. You can remember the things I've told you. But that doesn't mean—"

"Would I know that you always carry five single dollar bills in your wallet just in case a homeless person walks up to you and asks for money? Would I know you're scared shitless about planning Mira's wedding but you're going to do it anyway, not because you want the money, but because you already promised her that you would? Would I know that Amara isn't just a cousin to you, she's your best friend and your sister, and although you were happy for her when she got married, it hurt you a little inside because you knew you weren't the most important person in her life anymore?"

"How could you—" He took another step toward her. Only a few inches filled the space between them.

"Would I know that when you twist your hair around your finger like that, it's because you're trying to figure something out? Would I also know that when you're angry with me, you bite your bottom lip and when you're thinking about kissing me, you *also* bite your bottom lip?"

"I don't do that. Do I?" she said softly as he moved even closer. She realized then that he'd backed her up against the bedroom's wall.

He lowered his head and whispered, "You know what else I know? I know you want this." He savaged her mouth then, and it took only a second for her entire being to respond. She threw her arms around his neck, and he cupped her ass and lifted her up, pushing into her even more. "*Me vuelves loco*," he groaned.

"You drive me even crazier," she said against his lips.

"Why do we even bother fighting what's between us? *Sé que me deseas.*"

She did want him. There was no way she could deny it. He'd only have to touch between her legs to know just how much she wanted him. It was useless to fight what was so apparent, so obvious. She'd never been attracted to any man the way she was attracted to him. And he'd made it clear from the get-go that he wanted her whenever and wherever. Perhaps instead of stifling the fire, they should let the flames go wild? Eventually it would have to burn itself out, right? When it did, then she could walk away unscathed. It was time to turn this fake engagement into a very real sexual affair.

"I do want you. I don't want to, but I do," she finally admitted.

· · ·

Her words surprised him. He'd expected another denial, more questioning. Had she denied it, he'd dig deep and walk away… again. After all, he'd never had to convince a woman to sleep with him and he wasn't about to start now. Whatever doubts or fears she had going on in that beautiful head of hers, she'd have to figure out on her own eventually. At least for now, though, she wanted him just as badly as he wanted her. And he'd take it for as long as he could get it.

With her legs wrapped around his waist, he walked them over to the bed. She slid slowly down his body and the friction against his groin drove him wild with need.

He worked fast to pull off her T-shirt, exposing her bare, perfect breasts. He took one nipple in his mouth and groaned deep in his throat as he sucked and licked. "*Quiero devorarte,*" he whispered as he moved to the other breast.

The hunger he had for her was beyond anything he'd

experienced before. One taste wasn't enough. Ever. If anything, the more he touched her, licked her, the more he wanted. Yes, he'd devour every inch of her body tonight. He continued with her breasts, cupping them and circling her nipples with his tongue, taking time to flick the tips as she writhed against him.

"More, Brandon. I need more." Her voice, thick with desire, flared his want to new heights.

"Yes, baby. And I'm going to give it you." He lifted his head and found her mouth waiting and open. For him. Only him. And that was the way he wanted it from here on out. No more games for either of them. No more pretending that he couldn't wait to get home from New York because he wanted to give her the stupid ring and not because he wanted to see her, have her. Only her.

Although he hated to, he dragged his mouth away from hers so he could do more to her. Clothes were in the way, though. He tugged at her pants and they worked together to pull them off, along with her underwear. Then they moved to the side of the bed and got rid of his. Finally, they held each other skin to skin. The warmth of her body electrified his own, and his cock instinctively jerked into position. She noticed. Her small hand gripped his swollen erection and he swore in pleasure. As her hand continued stroking and squeezing his hard length, Brandon took her mouth again in one penetrating kiss. But not for long.

"You're going to make me explode if you keeping doing that," he said as he pulled out of her grasp. "So instead of me fucking your hand, how about I lie down and you get on top of me and ride me with that hot, tight pussy of yours?"

Her eyes flared, and he knew that's exactly what she wanted to do. He lay down and watched as she pulled out a condom from the bedside table drawer. He drank in the sight of her nakedness, from her perfect breasts down to the dark

V between her legs. He memorized the image, tucking it away in the back of his mind so he could call on it later if needed.

Shit. Even imagining himself imagining her as he stroked himself made his cock ache.

So when she finally sank down on him, he swore.

"Do you want me to go nice and slow, or hard and fast?" she asked, her eyes playful and teasing.

"Baby, I think we both want you to do me hard and fast."

She answered him by rising up then back down on him, over and over again. Her tempo picked up as he pushed into her deeper and deeper, and before long he watched her transform before his eyes. Her face darkened with the flush of desire, and beads of perspiration dotted her collarbone. And when she bit her bottom lip and threw back her head, he groaned. She looked so damn beautiful that he had to touch her and make sure all of this was real. Never in his life had a woman allowed herself to be with him like this. So free. So wild. He moved his hands up the side of her body and cupped and squeezed her breasts. She immediately grabbed onto his arms in order to use them for leverage and, God almighty, pounded him even harder.

"Yes, yes," she moaned between labored breaths. "Oh God, yes."

"That's right, baby. I can feel your pussy already clenching my cock. Let go for me."

"Brandon!" she screamed as her body convulsed on top of him.

The tremors triggered the beginning of his release, and he grabbed hold of her waist and bucked his hips. He held her still as he pumped into her two more times. Then he shattered into pieces, not caring how he'd ever become whole again.

Chapter Twelve

Brandon watched as the big hand of the wall clock finally landed squarely on top of the six. It was officially nine-thirty, and a full two hours since his mother had gone into surgery. He stood up from his seat in the hospital's waiting room, unable to contain his anxiety any longer. Shoving his hands into his pockets, he stalked across the small room and approached the silver-haired lady sitting behind the desk.

"Excuse me, ma'am, but do you have any update on Lorena Montoya?"

Although she offered him a polite smile, he could see her annoyance before she turned away to look at her computer screen. He didn't care if she was annoyed. Wasn't it her job to inform families about the status of their loved ones? It wasn't his fault the high-tech status-screen that usually showed the progress of a patient's surgery, via an assigned number rather than name, was on the fritz today. Although even if it had been on, he'd still be standing there, asking for news.

The woman turned back around and put on her fake smile again. "I'm sorry, Mr. Montoya, but there's still no new information since you asked me fifteen minutes ago."

"But it's nine-thirty and the surgeon said it shouldn't take more than two hours if there were no complications. And if there were complications, someone from his team would let us know. So why hasn't anyone let us know?" His tone, louder on his last sentence, made her raise her eyebrows. Again, he didn't care.

A hand touched his shoulder. "Brandon, I'm sure once there's something for her to tell us, she'll tell us. Right?"

The woman nodded at his sister. It irritated him that, as usual, she wasn't as concerned as he was. That was Alex, after all. He was the worrier of the family because he had to be. Otherwise bad things happened.

He moved away from Alex and stomped back to his seat. He caught Daisy's eye but looked away before she saw the fear that was thrashing his insides at that moment. Control was slipping from his grasp. He'd been grabbing onto it like a vice from the moment he woke up. This had been one of the hardest days of his life, yet he'd done everything he could to not show it, especially to his mom. He'd nearly lost it just before she was wheeled into surgery. He'd told her he loved her and when he bent down to kiss her forehead, she'd whispered that she loved him, too, and added, "If I don't come back, take care of your sister. And don't mess things up with Daisy. She's good for you."

Just thinking about it again made him choke on the emotion. He needed to get out of there before he exploded in either tears or anger.

"I need to make a call. I'll be back in a few minutes," he muttered to no one in particular and walked toward the small courtyard next to the surgery waiting room.

As soon as he got outside, he closed his eyes and sucked in the cool air. He could breathe again, and that started to calm him. Luckily, there was no one else on the patio and the tall hedges created a barrier between him and the parking lot on the other side. Finally, all alone, he wiped at the tears wetting his eyes.

A hand touched his shoulder, and he stiffened. "Look, Alex, I'm not in the mood right now to hear—"

"It's not Alex," he heard Daisy tell him.

He wiped his eyes again before turning around to face her. "Did the doctor come out yet?"

"No, not yet. I just came out her to make sure you were okay. If you'd rather be alone, I'll go back inside."

He'd thought he wanted to be alone. But now he wanted to be with Daisy. He grabbed her hand before she could leave. "No, stay with me."

She nodded. "I'm so sorry all of you have to go through this."

"Yeah, it sucks. But I guess it could be worse."

"You know she's going to be okay, don't you. She's a fighter. The doctor is going to take out the tumor and in a few months she'll be cancer free."

"Thank you."

"For what?"

"For telling me that. For being here with us. For agreeing to be my fiancée so she would have the surgery in the first place. For everything."

She shrugged and gave him a look that wrecked him. "I'm glad I'm here, too."

Fear and anger vanished. A new feeling overcame him, and that made him bend down to kiss her. Their lips met, soft and hesitant. There was nothing urgent or lustful about it. Yet it made his heart thump wildly in his chest and his gut clench. The sweetness of her mouth overwhelmed him, and for a few seconds the noise of cars and people coming and going on the other side of the hedges fell away. All he could hear were their mingled breaths, inhaling each other's need.

"Ahem. Excuse me, guys." Alex's voice cut through the heaviness of the emotion between them, and they pulled away from each other to look at her. "Sorry to interrupt, but the doctor's here and wants to talk to us."

Never letting go of Daisy's hand, he walked back inside with her and approached Dr. Katz, who still had his surgery scrubs and game face on. He didn't break it until all three of him were standing next to him.

"The surgery went extremely well. We were able to remove all of the tumor via laparoscopy so we didn't have to switch to the traditional open surgery. She's resting in the recovery room and you can go and see her in about half an hour. As long as we don't see any side effects from the anesthesia or the beginnings of an infection, she can go home in two days."

"When will she start her radiation therapy?" Alex asked.

"I'll know for sure after her follow-up appointment next week. But if all looks good she can start pretty quickly. I'm hoping so."

"Thank you, Dr. Katz. Really, I can't even tell you how appreciative we all are for taking such good care of her."

"You're welcome, Brandon. I've done my part. Now it's your turn to take care of her. You need to make sure she comes to all of her appointments and follows the diet that the nutritionist gave her. If she does everything she's supposed to, I don't see why she can't have a full recovery."

The doctor offered his hand and Brandon took it, the worry falling off his shoulders with every shake. When they were done, both Alex and Daisy gave the doctor a hug, which surprised but pleased him, judging by the big smile he wore when he finally left the waiting room.

But while Daisy was also smiling, Alex's face crumpled. He rushed to his sister's side and asked what was wrong.

"I'm just...so...relieved...she's...okay," she sobbed, and

then covered her face with her hands. He felt bad for ever thinking that Alex hadn't been just as worried as he had been. He pulled his sister into a bear hug and tried to comfort her.

"I'm going to go find her some water and tissues," Daisy told him, and left the room on her search.

He ushered Alex back to the row of black leather chairs that had been their home for the past few hours. She dug into her purse and pulled out a tissue. "I'm sorry for being such a crybaby," she said as she wiped her tears and cleaned her nose. "I just couldn't hold it in anymore."

"No need to apologize. Believe me. I almost had a breakdown outside before Daisy found me."

"Looks like she did a pretty good job of calming you down."

He caught the sarcasm behind her words and he smiled. If she was teasing, then she was feeling better. Although he'd usually respond with a smart comeback of his own, this time he couldn't think of one fast enough. Maybe because what she said was true. Daisy had calmed him and made him forget his anxiety for a few seconds.

"So you guys have gotten pretty close?"

"Well, we are pretending to be engaged."

"Um, there was no pretending going on as far as I could see. That kiss looked very real…and very hot." Again, what could he say? They sat in silence for a few seconds before she continued. "What are you doing, Brandon?'

"What do you mean?"

"What are you doing with Daisy? I thought this whole engagement business was supposed to be platonic. And sleeping together is exactly the opposite of platonic."

"Whoa, who said we were sleeping together?"

"That kiss did. And so did you just now by that reaction. Please, just be careful."

"Not that it's any of your business, but we are being

careful."

"I don't mean that, you dummy. I mean, be careful with her heart. Daisy has a really good one, and I'd hate to see it stomped on."

"Ouch. Thanks a lot."

"Look, we both know that neither of us do really well when it comes to long-term relationships. I have a tendency to pick guys that turn out to be blackmailers, and you have a tendency to pick women, well, who don't have the best intentions either. But Daisy's different. She's not the type of woman where you can just send a dozen roses to let her know you won't be calling anymore."

"Hey, I only did that once. And only because that was one was a little *loca*."

"That's my point. Daisy is kind and sweet and someday she's going to make someone very happy. And we both know that someone isn't going to be you. Is it?"

The thought of Daisy waking up next to some other guy every morning for the rest of her life annoyed him more than it should. And so did Alex's assumption that he was going to damage Daisy somehow. So what if he wasn't her Mr. Right? He'd never said he was. Plus, they'd both agreed that he'd be her Mr. Right Now while his mom was in town.

"Look, I appreciate you watching out for Daisy, but she's a big girl and she knows exactly what she signed up for. We know that this is just a temporary deal." Alex's raised eyebrow compelled a small confession. "Fine. I'm not going to lie. I like having her around, I like spending time with her and, yes, I like sleeping with her. But we were very clear about keeping our emotions out of it."

This time the arched eyebrow came complete with an eye roll. "Well, as long as you were clear about it…"

There was that sarcasm again. "What do you want from me, Alex?"

"Nothing. I just want to make sure that you're not kidding yourself about what Daisy may want from you eventually. Or even what you may want from her."

"I don't understand."

"Oh, dear brother. That's exactly what I'm afraid of."

Chapter Thirteen

"I don't like her."

Brandon leaned down to whisper in Daisy's ear. "You don't even know her. She seems harmless to me."

"That's because she's cooking you dinner," she whispered back. "I'm sorry, but you're kind of a manwhore when it comes to food."

He shrugged and acknowledged she was right. That made her smile, and she tipped her head against his shoulder. He moved his hand to cover hers and squeezed to let her know everything would be fine and that she needed to get over the fact that her dad had a girlfriend.

Her name was Teresa, and she was a widow he'd met during Bingo night at the church a few weeks ago. And now she was cooking them all enchiladas.

"It's just that I can't believe he didn't tell me about her before tonight. Don't you think I would deserve to know that he was seeing someone," she whispered as they watched the couple from the couch in her dad's living room. He was setting out plates on the kitchen table while Teresa was placing the silverware.

"He probably thought the same thing when you told him about us."

She turned away from the kitchen to look at Brandon. "You know that's different. Besides, it not like him to lie to me. Maybe that's her bad influence?"

"They're not teenagers you caught smoking," he said with a smile. "Yes, he invited us to dinner and neglected to mention that his new girlfriend would be joining us. That's not exactly lying."

"Well, it's not telling the whole truth either. I don't like it. And I don't think I like her."

They sat in silence for a few more minutes observing the very domestic scene.

"So he really has never had a girlfriend since your mom left?" Brandon finally whispered.

"Not that I remember. I guess he could have dated without me really knowing, but if he did, he never brought anyone home to meet me or cook dinner."

"Then he's been alone a long time, Daisy. Try to be happy that he found someone."

"Wow, Brandon. I thought you believed in lifelong bachelorhood?"

He shrugged. "I think it all depends on the person. If being in a relationship makes your dad happy, then I'm no one to judge. And neither are you."

Daisy thought about Brandon's words all through dinner. Her dad did seem to be smiling a lot more. He was even joking around with Brandon, which shocked the heck out of her since he hadn't been too happy that her supposed fiancé hadn't asked his permission to marry her—even if it would've only been a symbolic gesture since Daisy hadn't asked for his permission to do anything since she was seventeen. She knew she couldn't put off the meeting any longer, which was why she had said yes to coming over for dinner and why she'd dragged Brandon along.

Truth was, it was nice having him there.

"So Brandon, how is your mom doing?" her dad asked as they sat down to eat.

"Good, thank you for asking. She recovered pretty quickly from the surgery and is starting her first radiation therapy tomorrow."

"We'll light a candle for her at church on Sunday," Teresa added.

Okay, maybe she wasn't as bad as Daisy originally thought. The rest of the dinner went surprisingly well, and before long she realized her cheeks hurt from smiling and laughing so much.

"Teresa, these were some amazing enchiladas," Brandon said after nearly licking his plate clean. "Thank you again for cooking." He was always such the charmer, even around older women who smelled like *manteca* and Vick's Vapo Rub.

"Maybe she could cook some for your restaurant?" her dad asked.

Daisy tried hard not to roll her eyes. "Dad, Brandon's sister is the chef. I'm sure her enchiladas are the only ones they need."

"*Pues*, I just thought since your cousin sells her desserts there then maybe they needed some other dishes."

"Oh Juan, stop," Teresa said and leaned over to touch her dad on the arm. Daisy looked away. "My enchiladas aren't the kind people want to eat at a restaurant. They're too simple."

"Actually, Teresa, some of our most popular dishes are the simple and traditional ones that people grew up eating in their mother's kitchens. You'd be surprised," Brandon offered. "But I'm afraid my sister prefers to make all of the main dishes herself. She's a little bit of a control freak and doesn't let me bring in anything except Amara's desserts.

However, I definitely think your enchiladas are as good as any restaurant's."

Judging by the way Teresa's and her father's faces beamed with pride, she knew Brandon had just charmed his way into her family.

Well, her dad was the only family that counted anyway. Her mom had still been bugging her about wanting to meet him, but there was no way she'd subject him to that drama-mama.

In fact, none of Daisy's boyfriends had ever met her mother. Not even Luis. It helped that he was a garage mechanic—the kind of job her mother frowned upon. So she'd never asked to meet him and instead spent their three yearly phone calls telling Daisy that she could do better.

Who knew she'd be right?

But Brandon's not your boyfriend. And he'll never be part of your family. Why would he even want to?

As she listened to Brandon and her dad talk soccer while Teresa cleared the table, it was hard not to imagine what it would be like to have this perfect little picture for real. All that was missing was a couple of grandkids running around the living room.

Dear Lord, where'd that come from?

And she wasn't even drinking.

That's what happened when you grew up wishing you had a normal family like everyone else. Sure, she had friends whose parents were divorced, but she was the only one who lived with her dad. No one could understand why Daisy's mom wasn't around. And she was the last person who could explain it to them.

Her *abuela* and *tias* filled in here and there, and her poor dad did the best he could. But she was the one who taught herself how to cook and how to hem her own dresses, and when she got her period, she looked up what to do in a library book. Eventually she learned to accept the fact that her mom was more like a distant aunt she visited a few times a year.

She used to tell people that her childhood had made her stronger, more independent. What she didn't tell them was that it had also made it hard to rely on other people, or even trust that they truly wanted to be part of her life.

No wonder she'd given Brandon such a hard time.

As if he sensed she was thinking about him, he caught her eye and smiled. "What?" he mouthed as her dad searched the kitchen counter for a soccer magazine to show him.

She didn't answer because she didn't know what to say, how to describe what she felt when she saw him laughing at her dad's jokes and offering to help Teresa clean up.

It was such a drastically different picture compared to how she'd seen him before she'd stepped foot in that hotel bar.

They'd definitely become closer over the past few days, settling into a routine that involved more than just sex. Although the sex was still hot, they'd spend the hours afterward talking and teasing each other. Sometimes those were the moments that took her breath away. Fake engagement or not, they had turned into a couple. It felt nice. No, it felt better than nice. It was amazing.

But it's not going to last, the voice warned.

She knew that deep down. But for tonight, she wouldn't think about it. Instead, she'd enjoy spending time with Brandon, her dad and, yes, even Teresa, and pretend, for once, that she had a normal family just like everyone else.

Chapter Fourteen

Daisy checked her makeup one more time in her rearview mirror. Her dark, ruby-red lipstick and winged black eyeliner were as perfect as they had been when she'd left the house a half hour earlier. It wasn't a look she normally wore, but it was perfect for a special evening like tonight.

The valet attendant opened her door and helped Daisy out of her car. The bright lights of the L.A. Cuchara sign reflected off her windows even though the restaurant was technically closed for a private party. Some big movie producer was throwing himself a seventieth birthday bash, and the guest list was sure to be just as amazing as the food. Brandon and Alexa had worked themselves to the bone on the menu, Daisy had barely seen or spoken to him in days.

And a few days seemed like forever when all you wanted to do was touch the person you couldn't see.

He'd always text late at night to ask about his mom and ask about her, promising he'd wake her when he got home. But usually she'd find him the next morning passed out still in his clothes, either on the couch downstairs or in the other bedroom.

So when he'd mentioned in passing the other morning that she should come to the party, she decided to take him up on the invitation. Her first call was to Amara to see if she'd be able to stay with Lorena. She'd already been in radiation treatment for three weeks and the side effects had started to take hold. She was always tired and feeling sick to her stomach. Daisy didn't feel right leaving her alone even for a few hours, so luckily her cousin had agreed to come over. Once that was decided, she called Mira and asked if she'd go shopping with her to help her pick out the perfect dress. Credit card balance be damned.

As she walked through the front door of the restaurant, her stomach did flips worthy of an Olympic gymnast. But she knew her nerves had nothing to do with the immediate sightings of a few celebrities and everything to do with the thought of spending some quality time with a certain sexy restaurateur.

She grabbed a glass of champagne off a passing server's tray and gulped it down in the hopes it would calm her. Instead, warmth rushed to her head and she reached to steady herself on a nearby banister

"Daisy, is that you? Are you okay?"

She turned to see Dante, Brandon's lawyer friend, approaching her with a concerned look.

"Hello, Dante. Yes, I'm fine. Just drank my champagne a little too fast, that's all," she said and tried to laugh.

"Ah, okay," he laughed, too, and they exchanged polite kisses on each other's cheeks. Then he took a step back and she noticed an appreciative nod. He saw her watching him and he blushed. "Sorry, was I staring? I hope you don't mind me saying this, Daisy, but, wow. You look fantastic."

"Thank you. It's a new dress." Mira had picked it out, and at first Daisy had laughed at the thought of herself wearing something so revealing and tight. The red dress had a plunging neckline that made her cleavage appear much more bountiful than normal, and the clingy material accentuated her hips and ass. Mira had loved it on her so much that she threatened to buy it for her if Daisy didn't. Then her new friend and best client had surprised her that day with an at-home makeup and hair appointment with her own private stylist. There was no way Brandon was going to *not* notice her tonight.

She hadn't thought about other men noticing her, too. Dante must've sensed her wariness. "Don't get me wrong, that is quite a dress. But I meant everything about you looks great. I guess what I'm trying to say is that you look really happy, that's all."

Even though she'd been a little worried about not getting to see Brandon as much, she had to admit that she was genuinely happy. She'd landed a dream client and her event planning business was already drawing publicity and word of mouth referrals. Her dad had a girlfriend whom she suspected would soon be more. And she was having the best sex of her life with one of Hollywood's most eligible bachelors, and if things went as planned, she'd be having more of that amazing sex very soon.

"I am happy, Dante. I didn't realize until right now, but I am."

"Good. I'm glad to hear it. And, for what it's worth, Brandon has seemed pretty happy these days, as well."

"Really?"

"Of course. His mother's getting the treatment she needs, and we both know that it wouldn't have happened without you. I know he's very grateful to you."

Grateful wasn't the word she'd expected him to use when it came to Brandon's feelings toward her. She shook off the sudden dip in her own emotions and tried to change the subject.

"What about you, Dante? How are feeling these days?"

This time she'd expected a general "fine" or "good," not his very blunt, "Damn frustrated." She noticed him looking past her and turned her head to see who or what was at the other end of that highly intensive stare.

Alexa.

And then she understood. "Oh."

He dragged his eyes away from her and looked at Daisy again. "Yeah, oh."

"Well, don't give up just yet. Sometimes we get tired of pretending that what we want isn't what's right in front of us."

Wasn't that why she was here tonight? After a few days of not having Brandon in her bed, she decided she could do two things: pretend she didn't miss him and tell herself she didn't *need* multiple orgasms on a nightly basis, or get dressed up and do whatever it took to remind him what he'd been missing.

"I hope you're right. And, just so you know, it works both ways. Speaking of...I just spotted your fiancé, and judging by the stern look he's giving me, I think it's time for me to go find someone else to talk to. Enjoy the rest of your evening, Daisy."

She turned her head to follow Dante's gaze and saw Brandon's own gaze staring right back at her. It was as if she were seeing him for the first time, and what she saw took her breath away. He was dressed in a beautiful dark suit that accentuated his naturally tanned skin. His dark hair was slick and neat, and he was freshly shaven. But it wasn't just the way he looked—it was the way he looked at her. And although he was several feet away and across the crowded room, she felt his heat. Smelled his desire. Tasted his need.

Because they were the same as her own.

They made their way slowly to each other, stopping along the way to say hello to familiar faces, but only breaking eye contact for a few seconds. With every step, Daisy's nervousness fell away, replaced with a determined boldness to make it known how very badly she wanted him.

When they finally met in the middle of the room, every nerve hummed with a need that she'd never felt before.

"Goddamn, woman. You look fucking hot."

"Well, I figured if I'm supposed to be Brandon Montoya's fiancée, then I better look half as good as he does."

"Are you kidding me?" he lowered his voice and looked around the room. "You are the most gorgeous woman here, and if there weren't a hundred people in this dining room right now I'd bend you over the nearest table and show you just how hard I got the moment I saw you."

If she were telling the story later to Amara, she would've blamed the champagne. But in all honesty, it was the way he talked to her. And this time it was much more than the words—it was the raw need she heard behind them. It turned her on so bad that she decided to be as blunt as him.

"As much I'd love for you to do that, we can't obviously," she murmured into his ear. "But that doesn't mean we can't do something else."

Then she grabbed his hand and led him to his office.

She didn't say another word as they walked through the restaurant and then the kitchen. As people approached, he waved them off and said he had to take care of something and he'd be right back. When they finally made it inside and made sure the door was locked, he wasted no time in taking her into arms and plundering her mouth with his tongue.

"God, I've missed you. So much," he groaned between hungry kisses. His hands were all over her and she basked in his touch. But when his fingers traveled under the hem of her dress, she pushed them away.

"You don't get to touch me there...not yet."

He pulled away and looked at her with a surprised smile.

"Am I being punished or something?"

"Mmmm. You've made me wait for a few days, so I'm going to make you wait for a few more hours."

"I don't understand. Then why did you bring me back here?"

"So I could do this." She reached between them and cupped the hard bulge between his legs. On a groan, his eyes rolled back in his head. Daisy pushed him backward until his thighs hit the edge of his desk, then she undid his belt buckle and pulled his pants and boxers down to his ankles.

She took in the sight of his straining erection, and it thrilled her to know he was like that because of her. "I told you I was hard, baby," Brandon rasped. "I'm so hard it hurts, and only your mouth or your pussy is going to make me feel right again."

Forgetting about her expensive dress and perfect ruby lipstick application, Daisy dropped to her knees and took Brandon into her mouth. She heard him growl or groan, or both, above her. His reaction only fueled her own and she started to rethink her plan to withhold sex from him until later tonight. But as he muttered her name over and over again, she realized she was getting off on giving him so much pleasure.

"Damn, that feels so good. Do you like sucking my cock, baby?"

She hummed her appreciation and that seemed to make him go wild. He fisted some of her hair and his breaths grew ragged. She was drunk on desire and the overwhelming need to bring him to climax. She switched from sucking the length of him to licking around the tip of his penis, savoring the taste of him so much that she moaned as well.

"Holy shit, Daisy. I can't take much more. Fuck me one more time with that sweet mouth of yours so I can come."

Daisy did as instructed, not caring anymore that she

wasn't calling the shots. All that mattered was Brandon's release. And after a few more seconds, she got it. His thighs quaked under her grip as he exploded into her mouth, and she took everything he gave her.

When he was finally spent, he helped her to her feet and kissed her. When they broke for air, he tapped his forehead against hers and looked into her eyes. "That was fucking unbelievable. But tonight is going to be even better. Trust me."

He kissed her one last time before bending down to pick up his pants. She left him and headed toward his private bathroom where she knew she'd find extra toiletries like toothpaste and mouthwash. Unfortunately, it didn't have what she really needed: another set of panties, since the ones she wore were completely soaked through. She did the only thing she could do at that point.

When she was all cleaned up, she exited the bathroom and found a smiling Brandon waiting her for at the door.

"Guess I didn't mess up your hair and makeup too much. You still look fucking amazing."

His words brought a familiar rush of heat to her cheeks. Time to do the same to him. "Yeah, well, there was one thing I couldn't fix."

"And what was that?"

"My panties. I had to toss them into the trash, so you may want to get rid of them before the cleaning crew comes in."

"You threw them away? Then what are you wearing underneath?"

"What I plan to be wearing when you come home later tonight. Absolutely nothing."

She kissed him on the cheek and left him standing there with his mouth open and his complexion as red as her new shade of lipstick.

• • •

Technically speaking, Daisy had lied to him. She'd promised she'd be naked when he got home after the party. Instead, he found her on the bed still wearing the pair of strappy black heels she'd worn earlier.

"I still love the yoga pants look, but this is definitely a close second," he said after he closed and locked the bedroom door.

"I thought you'd like it," she purred, and his cock strained under his pants. He quickly remedied that by shedding all of his clothes and his socks and shoes. Then he joined her on the bed and took her into arms. They both groaned at finally having the skin on skin contact they'd been craving all night.

He kissed her hair, then her forehead, and finally her lips. He'd been thinking of them for hours now. How soft and warm they felt under his, and how hot and greedy they'd been around his cock.

"Do you know how difficult it is to be a good host when you've got a hard-on underneath your pants?" he asked her, as she moved her lips to kiss his jawline and neck.

"Probably as challenging as trying to listen to someone tell you all about their new car when you've got no undies on."

Her breasts jiggled against his chest as she laughed and he couldn't help thinking how wonderful that was. In fact, everything about tonight had been wonderful and it was only getting better. He lifted her chin to look at him, "You fucking rocked my world tonight, you know that? I don't know what I did to deserve that, but thank you."

"Honestly, it was supposed to be more of a punishment for staying away these past few nights. But I guess I didn't really think it through, did I?"

"Hey, I am sorry. You know I wanted to, right?"

It was the truth. Kind of. He *had* been busy working with Alex on getting the restaurant ready for the big party. But thoughts of a naked Daisy distracted him more than a few times, and he made himself stay away on purpose so he could concentrate on everything that needed to get done at work. Every time he saw her, though, it killed him to not reach out and touch her, or kiss her and hold her like he was doing now.

Then she'd walked into his restaurant looking the way she looked, and he knew he couldn't stay away any longer.

"None of that matters anymore. What matters is that you're here now," she whispered and his heart felt heavy with want. They kissed for a long time, reacquainting themselves with each other's taste and rhythm. Their tongues swirled and savored until it wasn't enough anymore.

He moved his mouth to her breasts and took one thick nipple gently between his teeth. Her sighs egged him on, and he longed to make her moan louder, harder.

"I need you in me now, Brandon. Please," she begged.

Nodding, he reached for the foil packet already lying on the bed. He quickly sheathed himself and then spread her open. The lips of her sex glistened, and an urge to taste her overwhelmed him. He moved down and settled between her legs. She groaned his name as soon as he slid his tongue against her opening. He swore and grasped her thighs and pulled them open even more. Then he licked her again and again until she pulled at his hair and bucked her hips.

"I'm going to come," she moaned.

"Then come," he rasped as he pushed himself back up, grabbed his cock, and penetrated her.

She swore as the orgasm rocked her body. As her pussy clenched him over and over, he bent down and captured her lips in an open kiss.

"*Somos uno*," he whispered into her mouth.

Thrust after thrust, they clung to each other. Moved together. And then came together one last time.

Afterward, once they'd both caught their breath, Brandon

hooked his arm under her and she snuggled against his chest. He kissed the top of her head and then inhaled. She always smelled so good. And he loved it that even when she wasn't with him, he could still smell her on him. He'd missed this.

"You feel so good lying next me," he told her. "I was an idiot for working so hard."

"You were busy getting ready for the party. I understand. I may not have liked it, but I understood."

"You do?" Daisy never ceased to surprise him. Most women would've been angry that he'd spent all his time at the restaurant. Not only was she not pissed, she'd given him a blowjob in his office.

Daisy sat up and pulled the sheet over her naked breasts. "This party was a big deal for your restaurant, right?"

"Huge. Big shots from the studio were there, and there was talk of getting us to cater their next awards dinner."

"Oh, wow. That's amazing. Congratulations. See, I get that. I get doing whatever it takes to get your hands on the next job. If all goes well with the wedding, then I'm going to get myself some office space so I can start meeting all my fancy new clients in places other than coffee shops and Amara's bakery."

He was impressed with her plans and a made a mental note to call his realtor friend and ask him to start looking into some rental properties for her. "That's a great idea. So, how are things going anyway, with the wedding planning?"

"Good, actually. Christian is a sweetheart. He just wants to do whatever Mira wants to do. If it were up to him, he'd marry her tomorrow at the courthouse. But Mira says she's only planning to get married once, and she wants to do it right."

"That's a nice thought." He crawled his fingers to the side of the sheet and tugged down.

"Why?" She swatted his hand away. "You don't think

their marriage is going to last?"

"I have no idea. But the odds are stacked against them. They're coming from two different worlds and Hollywood is rough on marriages."

"And fake engagements," she said with a laugh. Brandon joined in, thinking that this was exactly what he'd needed after the past few days. He wasn't even sleepy. He could talk and fuck all night if she wanted to.

He hoped she wanted to.

She reached over and rubbed his bare chest. The light touch of her fingers flipped a switch inside him, and his cock stirred from its short slumber. "Can I ask you a question?"

"Shoot," he answered, silently praying it had something to do with what position they were going to try next.

"Do you think if we would've slept together the night of Amara's wedding that any of this"—she pointed to him and then back to herself—"would have happened?"

That night seemed like a million years ago. It had changed so many things. Especially how he saw Daisy. In fact, it was hard to remember a time when she was just someone he worked with once in awhile. She'd become such a big part of his life since then. Actually, she'd become a part of him.

"I honestly don't know. I guess in a way it doesn't matter because we're here now. Right?"

She seemed satisfied with that answer and lay back down. She curled up next him, resting her head back onto his shoulder, and he kissed the top of her head. "Okay," she said. "I asked you something. Now it's your turn. Ask me anything."

Brandon smiled at the ceiling. "Have you bought any new yoga pants recently?"

Chapter Fifteen

Brandon sat in his car trying very hard not to throw his cell phone out the window. He counted to ten. He took deep breaths. He even closed his eyes and imagined the faces of puppies.

When it felt like his phone was no longer in danger, he turned off the car's ignition.

The conference call he'd just ended had come pretty close to being one of the worst in his career. Had he really just called Miami's planning commissioner a "prick who's lost his balls?"

He had.

Insulting one of the people you needed to approve your multi-million dollar project was probably an automatic rejection stamp. The Miami deal was as good as dead.

"Fuck. Fuck. *Fuck,*" he said as he bounced the back of his head off the driver's seat headrest. He cursed one more time before getting out of his car and walking up to the condo's front door. Before he opened it, he took another deep breath.

Push it down. Put it aside. Do whatever you have to do to forget about what happened for a little while.

It was time to celebrate his mom's last radiation treatment.

The past six weeks had flown by. The restaurant had been busier than ever, and, honestly, having Daisy around to take care of his mom's needs—and his own—had made the days and nights go faster. If he hadn't been dealing with all this bullshit with the Miami deal, he would've said the last two months hadn't been as painful as he'd feared. If anything—his mother's sickness aside—they'd been downright wonderful.

As soon as he walked through the door, the most incredible smell overwhelmed him. He recognized it in an instant.

Asopoa.

Light laughter danced from the kitchen, and he followed it and the wonderful smell.

"Oh, good, you're finally here," his mother announced as he entered the kitchen. She was standing at the stove stirring a large pot still on the burner.

"Hey there." Daisy appeared from behind her and moved to give him a quick kiss on the lips. "How was your day?"

He was thinking of how to respond when she touched his arm. "That bad, huh?"

"I'll tell you later," he whispered in her ear and stole another kiss. Then he walked over to his mom and kissed the side of her head. "I want to know how you're feeling, *Mamá*, but first I have to ask. Am I smelling what I think I'm smelling?"

She smiled proudly and nodded. "It is. But I didn't make it. Daisy did."

Brandon whipped his head around to look back at Daisy, who was now pulling bowls from a cabinet. "You made *asopao*?"

"You don't have to sound so surprised."

"Well, I mean, you've never, well, it's just that... Okay, yeah, I'm a little surprised."

His mother took the bowls from Daisy. "I wanted to make you a special dinner and Daisy suggested *asopao con pollo* and some *tostones*. But she didn't want me to tire myself out so I sat at the table and told her what to do, step by step."

The fact that she'd remembered how much he loved this dish warmed him as if he'd already taken a spoonful. She was full of surprises tonight, wasn't she?

"Okay, before we get all gaga over Daisy's cooking, it might be a good idea to actually taste it first," Daisy told him. "Your mom, and I say this with the utmost respect, was a drill sergeant with her instructions. But that doesn't mean I didn't find a way to fuu…um, ruin it anyway."

He laughed at her wide-eyed anxiety, and it loosened some of the knots tied in his neck and shoulders. When Daisy had called him earlier to make sure he could come home for a quick dinner, he'd actually gritted his teeth since he had the conference call planned with the commissioner. But now, standing in his kitchen, smelling the *asopao* and watching Lorena and Daisy chat as if they'd known each other forever, Brandon couldn't think of any place he'd rather be.

After pouring some of the *asopao,* with generous pieces of chicken into a bowl for him, Lorena filled two more for herself and Daisy. Then the three of them sat down at the kitchen table and dug in.

Brandon closed his eyes as the explosion of flavors hit his taste buds. The pieces of tender chicken and soft rice practically melted in his mouth amid the warm broth carrying the distinct tastes of tomato, peppers, garlic, and olive oil. The combination left him both satisfied and hungry for more. It still wasn't exactly his *mamá's asopao*. But that didn't matter. This version was Daisy's and that brought a comfort to him he'd never expected.

"Well?" Daisy's voice interrupted his savoring. He opened his eyes and saw her and his *mamá* staring at him, their spoons still on the table and their bowls untouched.

He carefully nodded in appreciation. "It's...good. Actually, it's pretty fantastic."

Both of the women sighed in relief and smiled at each other.

It wasn't until he was scraping the remnants in the bottom of his bowl that he remembered to also try the *tostones*. Once he did he was sorry that he hadn't enjoyed them with his soup. The twice-fried plantains were crispy and light with a dusting of salt and...maybe garlic? As soon as he finished his first one, he put his second one in his mouth and readied the third between his fingers.

"Oh, wow," he said with his mouth full. "These are so addictive. I think you need to make these every day, Daisy."

She grinned at him. "Again, all your mother. I was just the worker bee."

"He's right, Daisy," Lorena chimed in. "These are wonderful. Mine sometimes come out too salty or too oily. These are perfect."

Brandon nodded and popped a fourth into his mouth. "Okay, I'm ready for seconds. Anyone else?"

Both of them raised their hands.

About thirty minutes later, they had finally had their fill. Lorena went to her bedroom to lie down, and Brandon and Daisy cleaned up and put the leftovers away. As he watched her wipe down the table, a feeling of contentment drifted through him. And when she bent over in order to reach the center, another feeling zinged straight to his dick.

He moved behind her, grabbed her hips and pulled her ass against him.

She gasped and stood straight up. "What are you doing?" she whispered. "Your mom might walk in and see us."

"So? We're engaged remember? This is a perfectly acceptable way for engaged people to act."

"And when you turn around to talk to her, you'll be perfectly comfortable with her seeing what's making a dent in my back right now?"

Well, when she put it that way. "Fine. Then how about we go upstairs and get in the exact same position naked?"

"I thought you had to go back to the restaurant?"

"Haven't you ever heard of a quickie?"

She turned in his arms to face him. "You're always so romantic, aren't you?"

He laughed and pulled her into a hug. "Sorry. It's just that being inside you would really help me forget the shit that happened today."

"Uh-oh."

"Yeah, uh-oh. I'll spare you the ugly details. But let's just say I highly doubt Miami is going to be home to the new Cuchara restaurant."

Saying the words out loud gutted him. His failure was a bitter taste to swallow, especially after such a delicious meal. How could he have lost his temper like that? He knew better. He'd *done* better hundreds of times before. Why was this one call so different?

Because you were late for dinner.

It was true that he'd felt rushed to get off the phone because he knew Daisy and his *mamá* were waiting for him. Of course, they couldn't have known that he'd already had a ridiculously busy day or that he had to push off a few things in order to come home to eat. And it wasn't their fault that he'd agreed to it even though he knew he'd have to talk to the commissioner while he was driving.

But if he was still living as a bachelor with nothing or no one to come home to, he probably would've handled everything differently, starting by taking the call in his office with a stack of files to refer to whenever the commissioner asked him a question.

He knew better, and he should've prepared better. And he should've been more than just a little bit aggravated that Daisy had expected him to drop everything and come home just to eat a bowl of soup.

But he'd been having so much fun playing house the past few weeks that he'd let some of his focus and responsibilities slide. That couldn't happen anymore.

Brandon, realizing that he was still holding her, abruptly dropped his hands and stepped back. "It's getting late. I should go back to the restaurant."

Her puzzled expression did nothing to squelch his growing impatience. He had to get back to work. Why couldn't she understand that?

"You sure you're okay? If the day was as bad as you said, then why don't you take the night off?"

"It's my restaurant, Daisy. I can't just take the night off without making sure certain things are done and someone is there who can handle any emergencies."

"What about Alexa? She's there, too. Why can't you ask her to handle things?"

And that's when the wall he'd built to keep the day's annoyances at bay cracked. Hadn't he made it perfectly clear to her by now that his restaurants were his priority? And now that he'd let the Miami deal slip through his fingers and he'd more than likely lose his initial investment, it was more important than ever to make sure L.A. Cuchara continued to bring in money to the company. People were depending on him to make sure that happened. People like his *mamá* and Alex.

The words spilled out before he could stop them. "Are you serious? I'm sorry, but how many businesses do you have again? That's right. When your one business starts making the money that mine do, then maybe you can start offering me some career advice. Until then, I think I know what's best for my restaurants."

His tone was as harsh as it had been with the commissioner. At least he hadn't called her a name outright. Judging the by the redness of her face and her pinched expression he might as well have.

"God, Brandon. You really know how to convince someone *not* to have quickie with you. Go to the restaurant then. No one here needs you anyway."

With that, she threw the dishtowel she'd been using onto the table and stomped upstairs. Brandon swore under his breath so his mother wouldn't hear, headed out the front door, and got back into his car.

How dare she try to tell him how to run his business? Just because she was pretending to be his fake fiancée, and pretending to care about how he felt, didn't give her the right to butt her nose in where it didn't belong.

He was fuming as he pulled out of his driveway. But as he approached the exit gate for the community, the anger had begun to dissipate. The more he thought about the dinner she'd made and the way she'd laughed with his *mamá*, the more he realized that there were some things Daisy wasn't pretending.

She had been worried about him and had only tried to help.

Brandon pulled over to the curb, turned off the ignition, and closed his eyes.

Maybe the planning commissioner had acted like a prick. But it turned out that Brandon was the biggest one of them all.

• • •

Daisy stepped into the shower and hissed as the hot spray made contact with her skin. The temperature hovered between painful and perfect. It was exactly what she needed to help distract her from the torpedo of emotions Brandon had launched with his tirade downstairs.

That was the last time she'd ever ask about his restaurant issues again. And definitely the last time she'd work so hard to cook him dinner. From now on he could eat at the restaurant by himself. Hell, he could even sleep there if he wanted to. Why the hell should she care?

She hated to admit how badly his words had stung. Instead she'd rather stand under the stream of water as it washed her embarrassing tears away. She forced herself to concentrate on her lunch meeting with Mira tomorrow. They were going to finalize a list of possible wedding locations. Thinking about that and some other pending contracts helped her regain some sense of control.

So what if Brandon didn't appreciate everything she'd been doing lately? She didn't agree to this fake engagement in order to be a confidante or partner. She'd done it to make her own business a success.

Stop worrying about him so much and focus on what's best for you. That's all that matters anyway.

Daisy had been so wrapped up in her thoughts that she didn't hear the shower door click open. So she jumped when Brandon said her name.

"Holy shit!" she yelled and whipped around. He was standing in the shower with her, naked and looking grim. "What the hell are you doing? You scared the crap out of me. I thought you left."

He didn't answer her with words. Instead, he moved and wrapped his arms around her wet body and pulled her into him. Her anger from before returned. If he thought she was in the mood for a quickie now, after everything that had happened, he was going to have a rude and very uncomfortable awakening.

She left her arms at her side and stiffened her back. The

hot water pelted them as they stool in silence for what seemed like an eternity. Despite her determination to stay unaffected, her body started to betray her. Her nipples pebbled against his hard chest and her sex tightened as his thick erection pressed into her belly. Her willpower weakened with every second until she couldn't take it anymore and finally slid her arms around his back.

She felt his body sag, and he squeezed her tighter. "I'm so sorry. I'm a giant ass. Please forgive me."

The tears fell again and she was grateful that water still rained down her face. He couldn't know how he'd hurt her. "It's fine. You don't owe me an apology. You don't owe me anything," she said, and pressed her cheek against his upper arm.

He rubbed circles on her back and kissed the side of her head. "I owe you everything, Daisy."

"I shouldn't have pressed you to come home tonight. You obviously had bigger things to worry about than a stupid dinner. It won't happen again."

"Stop." Brandon maneuvered them out of the shower spray and pulled away so he could look at her. "Stop, okay? You have every right to be pissed off and hurt. You did something nice for me and I basically crapped all over it. Yes, I had a busy and fucked up day. But coming home to eat one of my favorite dishes with two of my favorite women kind of made it all better. You made it all better, and I'm sorry that I never said thank you."

She looked into his eyes and could see he meant every word. God, she was such a sucker for heartfelt apologies, especially when they were made by gorgeous men who were holding her naked.

"I'll forgive you on one condition."

"Anything," he said. "Just name it."

Daisy reached up and settled her hands on his broad shoulders. "Kiss me."

Brandon groaned before slamming his lips onto her hers. She felt his hands move down her back to grab her ass. Throaty sighs escaped from both of them as he palmed and squeezed each cheek, grinding himself against her slickened upper thigh. Shivers traveled down her back despite the warm sprays of water still splashing against it.

He lowered his lips to her ear. "Let's get clean now so we can get very dirty later." He reached behind her to grab the bottle of shampoo sitting on the shower rack. With a flick of his thumb, he popped open the top and took a sniff. "Strawberry?"

"Berries and other natural botanicals," she quoted.

"Whatever it is, I love the way it makes your hair smell. Turn around."

She obeyed and waited with bated breath for his next move. A cool drip slid down the back of her head, filling the enclosed space with a sweet combination of fruity fragrances. Daisy closed her eyes as Brandon began massaging the shampoo into her hair, lulling her into a relaxed stupor. When it was time to rinse, she moved only because Brandon moved her. She murmured something about conditioner and he seemed to understand. Soon his magic fingers were back in her hair and she turned to mush all over again.

But her body zinged back to life as soon as she felt hot, soapy hands on her shoulders.

"What are you doing now?" she asked and looked up at him with a half smile.

"It's time to wash your body," he said, both serious and teasing.

"You know, the loofah pad is right over there in the corner."

"I'm more of a hands-on type of guy, if you know what I mean."

And in case there was any doubt, he slid his palms down

to her chest until they cupped her breasts. Then he began to rub.

Her nipples puckered in response to the glorious pressure and she gasped. Drops of water trickled inside her mouth and she instinctively licked her lips. Then Brandon licked them too.

"Sorry, I couldn't resist. Now, back to washing," he murmured.

As promised, he continued to lather the rest of her chest and stomach before moving to arms and back. With each stroke on her skin, he stirred a fire beneath it. She was sure her core temperature burned hotter than the water by now.

She wondered if she could take much more.

"Put your right leg on the bench seat," he said, his voice rough and thick.

She did again as he commanded. Did she really have a choice? His touch, the intimacy of the moment, had made her drunk on her own arousal. All she could do was blush. No man had ever done anything like this to her before. She felt worshipped.

Brandon knelt on one knee before her and languidly slid his lathered palm from her ankle up her calf, rotating his wrist to ensure he soaped every inch. He moved to the top of her thigh and it trembled back. But when his fingers slid underneath it, her entire body shuddered in pleasure.

"Oh my God," she breathed.

He switched hands and brushed soap over her other leg. She watched from above, entranced and enflamed all at the same time as he took his time to generously lather her. And when he finally moved his hands to between her legs, she was rendered speechless.

Brandon slid his fingers across her folds. Back and forth. Side to side. His touch was light but devastating. Without thinking, she began to move her hips to his rhythm.

"Fuck, Daisy. Do you know I much want to suck this

beautiful pussy?"

The rawness of his voice made her ache, *ache*, with need.

"I do," she said, surprised by the deepness of her own tone, "because it's probably as much as I want you to."

He looked up at her and their eyes locked in a flash of mutual desire. Daisy was so turned on she was ready to do whatever he wanted. The man could've asked for anything and not only would she do it, she would thank him later for the privilege.

Instead, he stopped touching her and stood up. Before she could collapse in disappointment, Brandon put his hands on both sides of her head and found her lips. Their mouths opened so their tongues could lick and play with each other.

Daisy's arms circled his neck. Her head spun as Brandon's taste mingled in her mouth with sprinkles of water. How on earth had she come to be in this place, in this moment? Girls like her didn't have sex like this. Okay, technically this wasn't sex, but it was damn fucking close. Never before had she felt so wanted, so lusted after.

She could so get used to this.

Their kisses turned frantic, demanding. And the harder and faster they kissed, the more she realized she'd never be satisfied until another part of him was inside her.

She let go of his neck and slid her palms down the front of his chest then gently nudged him back. "Your turn," she teased.

Hunger flared in his eyes and they traded spots under the showerhead. When he saw her reach for the bottle of shampoo, he lowered his head without her having to ask. His hair was too short to thread her fingers through, so she used both hands to smooth the white, creamy liquid all over and then gently started to scrub.

"God, that feels so good," he said on a moan.

"I know," she said with a smile.

When she was satisfied, she told him to turn around and rinse. She opened the body wash and squirted the soap into her left palm and waited for him to finish.

"Stay facing that wall," she instructed. When he told her he was ready, she rubbed the body wash between her hands and began lathering his back. She started near his shoulders and spread the soap with fanned fingers. His slickened skin was smooth but it didn't detract from the firmness of the muscles underneath. No wonder he could lift her like a kitten.

When his upper back was all nice and soapy, she slid her hands under his arms and pressed her breasts against his back. From behind, she spread the body wash around his chest and made sure to pass over his hardened nipples again and again.

"Oh, yeah, baby. You feel so good. This all feels so good," he whispered.

Part of her wanted to reach for his stiff, jutting erection. Daisy couldn't see it from her current position but she knew it was there. She could sense it.

You should save the best part for last.

As her reward for her willpower, she moved her hands to the second best part of Brandon's body—his firm, tight ass.

He gasped. "Son of a bitch. Damn, I love when you touch my ass."

She wasn't just touching it, though. She was kneading it, caressing and adoring it. And when she boldly traced the cleft in the middle, Brandon lurched forward and spun around. "Okay, that's it."

"But I didn't even do your legs," she protested.

"I didn't say we were done. Not even close. Put out your hand."

Although she was still confused, she put out her hand. Her grabbed her wrist and squirted more body wash onto her palm. Then he moved her until her back touched one of the shower's tiled walls.

"Are you ready?"

"Ready for what?"

"My cock is going to fuck your hand and that tight pussy of yours is going to fuck my fingers."

He pushed her hand down between them and maneuvered himself until she could take hold of his erection. At last.

She started stroking him but stopped when he sucked on a nipple and slid two fingers inside her.

"Ahhh," she moaned.

"Keep moving your hand, *amante*. I'm so worked up it's not going to be too much longer. And judging by how slick and hot you are, I have feeling you're right there with me."

She was. Her release had been tightening in her stomach since the moment she touched him. She was ready to come. God, she was ready. But she wanted him to come more.

And so she picked up her pace, curling her fingers firmly around his engorged shaft, pulling up and pushing down, making sure to grasp the tip in every rotation. Meanwhile, Brandon was just as focused, alternating between finger thrusts and rubbing circles along the tight bundle of nerves that held the key to her final undoing.

Their breaths turned ragged. Their movements became frenzied.

Pull and thrust. Pull and thrust.

"Fuck. Yes. Fuck."

Daisy looked down and watched as Brandon pumped into her hand over and over again. It was all she needed.

Every muscle in her body tensed as if suspended in time. And then the moment shattered, sending everything she'd ever felt crashing to the ground in magnificent pleasure.

Brandon's own groans brought her back from nirvana just in time to witness his body stiffen after one last pump. Warmth and wetness covered her hand as he shouted her name and slumped against her.

Chapter Sixteen

"I don't know. Is it just me or does that bush look like it's been shaped into a giant penis?" Mira asked.

Daisy shielded her eyes from the sun and followed Mira's pointing finger. "No it doesn't... Oh my God, it does!"

Daisy and Mira looked at each other and laughed before surveying the rest of the garden landscape at the Downtown Los Angeles Library. When Mira had first told her where she wanted her wedding to take place, Daisy had kept her reservations to herself. Apparently this was where Christian and Mira had shared their first kiss, so she went along with the sugary sweet fantasy, secretly making a list of alternate locations until they were thrown a curveball. Filming on Christian's first movie was unexpectedly moved up, which meant the wedding had to be rescheduled. And since the library had already been booked well into next year with other events, it seemed like Daisy's backup list would come in handy after all. But then the event coordinator called last week and said a cancellation had opened a date for next month.

She didn't know whether to laugh or cry when she heard the news. How could she possibly pull together a wedding in less than thirty days? But as they walked around the beautiful grounds and talked to the event coordinator, Daisy's doubts began to fall away, and all kinds of ideas popped into her head. The excitement on Mira's face alone told her that this was the perfect place to have the wedding. Because of that, she was willing to overlook a penis-shaped shrub.

"Don't worry, my friend," Daisy said. "On the day of the wedding we can put one of the columns right in front of it. No one will notice it at all. Especially, when you come walking down that aisle."

"Ah, you're such a kiss-ass. Thanks again for being so flexible with everything. Did you end up rescheduling your doctor's appointment?"

The appointment actually wasn't hers to reschedule. Today was the day Lorena was going to find out if she needed any more treatments. Dr. Katz had told them at her last appointment that if the PET scan showed anything, they'd have to regroup and talk about another round of radiation and perhaps even chemo.

"The appointment was for Brandon's mom. They went ahead without me."

"Oh my gosh, Daisy. Why didn't you tell me? I totally would've tried to get us an appointment later in the week."

"It's okay, Mira. Brandon insisted that I come with you today instead. He knows how important it is to you and Christian to get married here, and if we'd rescheduled there was a very good chance another opening wouldn't come up here until the end of next year."

"Well, that's very understanding of him. Hey, speaking of wedding locations, have you guys picked yours?"

And now came the part that Daisy always hated—lying to Mira about her engagement to Brandon. She was a bride-to-be so it was natural for her to want to talk bride stuff like flowers and cakes and place settings. She involved Daisy in more than the usual wedding planner decisions, and Daisy had begun to feel guilty about it.

"Oh, you know, we're still talking it out. We figure we still have some time."

"Don't tell me you guys are going to be one of those couples who are going to be engaged for ten years before you just decide one day to take a trip to city hall?"

As if. "Nope. I have a feeling our engagement won't be lasting that long," she said. It was a half-lie—or rather a half-truth. Either way it made it her sick to her stomach not to be able to confide in Mira about what was really going with her and Brandon.

Although, she didn't quite know what was going on with them, either. They'd spent almost every night together in the same bed, and when he couldn't come home for dinner, she and Lorena would go the restaurant to meet him and Alexa. They'd gotten into quite a comfortable routine and not just with his family. There'd been other outings with her dad and Teresa, and evenings out together for a movie premiere or charity fundraiser. They had become the perfect fake couple— so much so that she'd begun to wonder what it would be like if they weren't pretending.

The only problem? Brandon seemed perfectly content with the way things were.

As Mira went off to go find the event coordinator, her thoughts drifted back to Lorena. She'd grown so close to her in the past several weeks. Daisy smiled thinking of the first time they'd met and how uncomfortable she'd felt around the loud, boisterous woman. It had been a privilege to go with her to her radiation appointments and take care of her in the evening while Brandon was at the restaurant. To her credit, she never pressed Daisy about her relationship with her own mother, seemingly satisfied with her response that it was "complicated."

Some of her most favorite moments had been when the two of them would run errands together and talk about her life in Puerto Rico and how Brandon had been as a kid. The pride and adoration in Lorena's eyes when she spoke about her son melted Daisy's heart night after night.

She had to be okay.

Please God. Let her be okay.

She looked at the time on her phone and figured they should already be in with Dr. Katz. Soon they'd all know if their prayers had been answered.

. . .

Daisy walked into L.A. Cuchara and headed toward the back. It was packed, but even as the waiters and waitresses rushed from table to table, they all stopped to say hello. One girl she didn't recognize even called her Mrs. Montoya.

She must be new, Daisy thought. Rather than correct her, she smiled and said hello back. The giddiness she felt at the thought of being mistaken for Brandon's wife disappeared the moment she opened the door to the back office.

Whatever Alexa, Lorena, and Brandon had been talking about stopped when they saw her. She met Brandon's eyes for a second before he looked away. Her chest tightened, and she held her breath for the bad news.

Lorena stood up, walked over to Daisy and pulled her into an embrace. She didn't hesitate this time and hugged her back as hard as she could. "Tell me," she whispered.

Lorena pulled away and that's when Daisy noticed that she was smiling. The older woman took her hands and squeezed. "The cancer is gone. *Gracias a Dios.*"

She grabbed Lorena and hugged her again. Tears of relief

finally spilled onto her cheeks and she buried her head into Lorena's shoulder. "I'm so happy for you. For all of you."

After they hugged for a few seconds, Daisy pulled away and wiped her eyes. She looked at Alexa, whose face was beaming, and then at Brandon, who still wore a sullen expression.

What was wrong with him?

"I think we need to celebrate," she gushed. "How about tonight?"

"Before we celebrate… *Mamá*, tell Daisy the rest of your news," Brandon finally said.

Daisy looked at Lorena. "There's more?"

"Yes. The doctor says I can go back to Puerto Rico. We just bought my ticket. I'm leaving this Saturday."

She looked at Brandon. This meant their arrangement was ending. The deal had always been to tell Lorena that they decided to call off the wedding once she went back home. That way both of them would be safe from her wrath in person.

"Oh. So soon? What about your follow-up appointments?"

"I'll come back to L.A. every couple of months. It will be fine. And guess what? I have more good news!"

By the look on Brandon's face, she doubted it. Even though she was afraid to, Daisy asked anyway.

"I called the church where I was married and the priest says you can get married there," she gushed. "I know you haven't set a date yet, but I don't see why we can't have the wedding in Puerto Rico."

Her heart practically stopped. "Oh, Lorena. I…um…I don't know what to say."

"See *Mamá*, I told you she wouldn't want to get married in Puerto Rico."

Daisy frowned at Brandon. Why was he putting this all on her? "It's not that I'm saying no, it's just that I'm so busy planning Christian and Mira's wedding that I think it's going to be a while before I can even start thinking of planning ours."

The older woman nodded wildly. "Yes, of course. I know you both are very busy. How about this? Why don't you both come after their wedding so we can go see the church?"

Daisy still didn't know what to say.

And Brandon, of course, still wouldn't help. "Yeah, right," he muttered.

"What's that supposed to mean?" she asked, and looked over at him.

"It means how are we going to go see a church in Puerto Rico if you refuse to fly there."

His mother furrowed her eyebrows. "Why won't you fly there?"

"Because she's afraid the plane will crash," Brandon answered for her. "And she won't take a boat either because she somehow thinks she'll end up sharing one bathroom with hundreds of sick people."

"I don't understand," his mother looked at Alexa, who simply threw up her hands.

Daisy's cheeks burned. She was going to have a few choice words with Brandon later about putting her on the spot like this. "Okay, maybe I'm a little bit afraid. But there are some good drugs I can take to knock me out or something, right?"

Even though she'd said them, Daisy couldn't believe the words that had just come out of her mouth. It was Brandon's fault. If he hadn't teased her, she wouldn't have tried so hard to prove him wrong. Now, all she'd done was manage to tell Lorena another lie. There'd be no need for knockout drugs because there'd be no need for her to get on a plane because there'd never be a wedding. The fake engagement was coming to an end.

The disappointment in her gut rattled her. Before it could show on her face, though, she plastered on a smile and took a deep breath. She might as well just dig her hole a little deeper. In a few days, none of this would matter anyway. "I'll be fine. If it means this much to you then we'll figure it out. I'll come to Puerto Rico."

Lorena squealed in delight and clapped her hands. Then she went over to Alexa and they began chatting about all the places they were going to take Daisy to visit in Puerto Rico.

Brandon got up from his chair and walked over to Daisy.

"What the hell was that?" he asked.

"She caught me off guard with the church thing. And then you didn't help things by basically challenging me to get on a plane."

"I was trying to give you an out."

"Oh. Well, next time do it better."

"You know she really thinks you're going to Puerto Rico now?"

"I know and I feel bad. I'm sorry."

"I think we should talk about…things. How about we go out tonight, just the two of us?"

A night out with Brandon sounded both wonderful and scary. His mom was going back to Puerto Rico. There was no need to pretend to be engaged anymore, and she wasn't quite sure yet how she felt about that. But if this thing with Brandon was about to end, then she'd take every last minute of it.

"Okay, dinner sounds nice."

He smiled at her and then turned to ask Alexa a question. And as the conversation changed from Puerto Rico to other random topics, Daisy stood there and tried to ignore the feeling of dread bubbling inside her stomach.

• • •

Brandon couldn't help but feel nervous.

He sat at the table waiting for Daisy to return from the

ladies' room. They'd just arrived at the restaurant when she excused herself. Now as he sat there, he tried to come up with the right way to say what he wanted to say when she came back.

As soon as his *mamá* told him that she wanted to go home to Puerto Rico right away, he knew that meant that things with Daisy were coming to an end. And up until that moment, he'd been preparing for it. Had been resolved to it. But now the thought of never having her in his bed again… kind of pissed him the hell off. And that's when it hit him. For all intents and purposes, this had been a business deal. And what did he usually do when he wanted a better offer? It was time to renegotiate.

He looked up in time to see her walking toward him. Although she'd looked apprehensive earlier, her face was bright and beaming now. She sat down across from him and he grabbed her hand and brought it to his lips. "You look beautiful tonight," he said before kissing her hand softly.

"Thank you. You look pretty nice yourself. Is that a new suit?"

He loved that she noticed things like that. "It is. I bought it just for our date."

"Oh, this is a date?"

"Of course. I'm prepared to wine and dine you for a few hours and then we'll have some dessert later. If you know what I mean."

She rolled her eyes and laughed. "I told you before. I always know what you mean."

They sipped their drinks and discussed what to order. He'd brought her to this hole-in-the-wall Italian restaurant just a few blocks away from the condo. Far from a Hollywood hot spot, the restaurant was still packed with diners, and he knew that meant the food was as good as he'd heard. The cozy dining room and quaint decorations, including strings of twinkle lights wrapped around pillars, screamed family-owned. He knew that Daisy would love it.

And judging by the big smile on her face and the way she ooh'd and aah'd over the menu, he'd been right.

After the waiter left with their orders, he knew it was time to discuss terms.

"I'm so glad we're doing this. I think it's better that we discuss things away from the house and away from *Mamá*. She's been talking nonstop about everything she's going to do once she gets back home. She's starting to feel like her old self again. I can already see it."

"Well, a huge weight has been lifted off her shoulders… and yours. I'm so happy for all of you." Daisy reached across the table and squeezed his hand.

"You know I couldn't have gotten through this without you, right? I'll never forget what you did for her, for my family. Thank you again."

"You're welcome. I still think we need to celebrate."

He nodded. "Definitely. How about we all go to dinner on Friday night?"

"But isn't that your busiest night? What about the—"

He let go and waved his hands to stop her. "It's a special occasion. I'll make the arrangements and we can even go eat a little earlier just in case I end up having to head in later that night."

Daisy took a sip of her wine. "Then let's do Friday. I have a meeting in the morning with the florist and then a doctor's appointment in the afternoon, but I should be done with everything by three or four."

"Doctor's appointment? Everything okay?"

"Oh yeah," she said with a quick nod. "It's just a regular physical. No biggie."

"Good, I'm glad. Then Friday it is. I know my *mamá* will be happy that we're all going out together."

She smiled at him and he took a breath. It was now or never. "You know, when my *mamá* goes home, we can still have nights out like this together, just the two of us. Would you want to do that?"

She held his gaze, but he couldn't decipher her emotions from her eyes alone. The longer she took to answer, the more anxious he became.

"What are you saying, Brandon?" she finally asked.

"I'm saying I like being with you, Daisy. And you *know* I love sleeping with you. So I propose another extension to our original agreement."

"You still want to pretend to be engaged?"

"Sure. Why not?"

"Um, because your mom isn't going to be around."

"Not here in L.A., but she's not going to stop wanting to talk to you about the wedding. What do you want me to do? Tell her we broke up the minute she lands in Puerto Rico?"

"No, of course not. I figured we'd give it some time. I've grown to care for your mom. I don't want to do anything that's going to hurt her or make her hate me."

"Why would she hate you? If anything, she's going to blame me for our breakup."

Daisy laughed and he relaxed. "I can't believe we're actually talking about our fake breakup."

"Well, you're the one who agreed to go see that church for our fake wedding that's going to happen in Puerto Rico."

She sighed and shook her head. "This charade has kind of spiraled out of control, hasn't it?"

"It's become more than what I thought it would be," he said and reached across the table to grab her hand again. "But it can still be even more, if you agree to my proposal."

Daisy had proven to be his match both in and out of the bedroom. She challenged him in so many ways, and he liked to think that he'd had a positive effect on her life as well. So why did they have to put an end to a good thing? They'd spend their days taking over the world and spend their nights taking over each other's bodies. He had been right that she'd been the perfect woman to be his fake fiancée. Their business deal had benefitted both of them. It made perfect sense to explore the option of continuing it.

Why didn't she seem as convinced?

He sat back in his chair and folded his arms across his chest. "All I'm saying is that we keep things status quo for a while. Or are you in a rush to move out or something?"

"No. I guess not."

"Then what's the big deal? We're consenting adults who like having sex but aren't interested in a real romantic relationship because we're both too focused on our careers right now. It's the best of both worlds, isn't it? So we keep up the charade for a little while longer for everyone's benefit. Then we can reassess in a few weeks and decide if it's been enough time to implement the next phase of our arrangement. We can call it Project Pretend Break-Up."

The name had come to him on the drive over and he'd thought it was funny. He still did and chuckled. But he stopped when he saw the blank expression on her face.

"Wow. You've really given this some thought."

Did he detect a hint of bitterness behind her words? Although he knew there was a possibility, he hadn't really expected her to turn him down. Their relationship may have started off on shaky ground, but things between them lately were good. Very good. At least he thought so. Had he misread her?

"Look, this is just an idea. You've more than fulfilled your end of the original deal, so of course I'm not going to stop you from moving out of my house…or out of my bed if that's what you want. What *do* you want, Daisy?"

Something flashed behind her eyes but she looked away

before he could read anything into it. He took a gulp of his wine and then leaned back and waited for her response.

Seconds seemed like hours. Finally she looked at him again, and his heart quickened just like it did whenever he was about to close a big deal.

"I want to stay," she said with a nod. "But just for a few more weeks, okay? I think it will be too sudden to tell Lorena anything earlier than that, and she needs to focus on her recovery, not on our supposed breakup. But I also don't want to keep deceiving her any longer than we need to. So, yes, I agree to your proposal to extend our arrangement for a little bit longer."

Brandon should've been thrilled. He'd gotten what he wanted. His adrenaline should've been pumping as if he'd just landed a huge contract. Sure, he was happy. But there was something holding him back from feeling totally satisfied.

Halfway through his Linguine Puttanesca, it finally came to him.

Daisy had agreed to keep pretending they were engaged because of Lorena. She hadn't said one word about wanting to stay because of him.

Maybe he'd been wrong about her after all.

Chapter Seventeen

Daisy looked again at the fuzzy white blob on the paper. Through her tears, it only looked more distorted, almost like one of those black and white drawings psychiatrists showed their patients to diagnose their problems.

What did it mean then that she could only see a white, alien-looking blob on that paper instead of a baby? Her baby.

Brandon's baby.

She wiped her eyes just as Amara sat down across the table from her. They were meeting at a coffee house just down the street from Amara's bakery. No way were they going to have this conversation where there was a chance Amara's parents could show up unexpectedly. "Okay. I'm here now. Oh, honey. Are you crying again?"

Daisy attempted to smile. "Again? I don't think I've stopped since I found out."

Her cousin grabbed her hand. "So tell me everything that happened."

Despite the tears on the outside, Daisy's insides were full of love and gratitude that Amara had dropped what she was doing to meet her.

"It was supposed to be my regular annual exam. The nurse came in to take all of my vitals. She asks me about the last time I had my period and I can't remember. But that's not unusual because, you know, I've never been regular while taking the birth control shot. So I kind of laugh it off and she asks if there's a chance I could be pregnant." Her voice broke, and she looked out the window. People walked by, going about their normal and simple lives. She envied them.

Her life was going to be anything but.

She cleared her throat and looked back at Amara. "Anyway, they took a pregnancy test and it came back positive and then I demanded they do a blood test, too. And about an hour later, the doctor called me back into her office and told me the first test was right. Of course she sees my engagement ring and tells me congratulations, and I just lost it right there in front of her."

Her cousin shook her head. "This doesn't have to mean the end of the world. You're not alone. I'm going to help you through this. No matter what you decide."

"Thank you, *prima*. I don't know what I'd do without you. And now I'm going to start crying again," she squeaked before reaching for more napkins.

"Stop. You're going to make me cry and I'm not even pregnant," Amara said.

Daisy handed her a napkin and they both sat there for a few seconds blowing their noses and dabbing their eyes. She knew people in the coffee house were staring at them. And why wouldn't they? They were a pair of blubbering women crying over a plate of uneaten scones.

She looked again at the sonogram image and shook her head. "How did this happen?"

Amara raised her eyebrow.

"Yes, I know *how* it happened. I guess I just can't believe that it did."

They'd been so careful, so purposeful in using condoms even though she'd been on birth control. She'd even told the doctor that as if she needed to somehow prove she wasn't some naive teenager. The doctor had only shrugged and repeated statistics about condoms failing, and the fact that Daisy had been a few weeks late in getting her next shot. The ridiculousness of it all should've made her laugh. Instead, it made her cry more.

"Do you know what you're going to do yet?" her cousin asked.

She did. As soon as the first test came back, she knew. "I'm going to keep it."

Amara grabbed her hand again. "Are you sure?"

"I am. In fact, it's the only thing I'm sure of."

"And Brandon?"

She exhaled, as her chest seemed to compress on its own. "I have to tell him. As soon as possible. And then I guess we'll go our separate ways."

"Maybe not?"

Daisy couldn't help but snort. "Have you even met Brandon? Can you honestly tell me you can see him trading in his Jaguar for a mini-van, or holding PTA meetings in the dining room of L.A. Cuchara? He loves being a bachelor— he's told us that a million times. The last thing I want is for him to feel forced or tricked into being a dad. So I'm going to tell him that he doesn't have to be involved."

She cringed at the thought of having to have such a conversation. If Brandon hadn't wanted a relationship with her a few days ago, he definitely wasn't going to want one now. He still saw what they were doing as nothing more than a business deal. Sex with no strings attached was his calling card. She shouldn't have been surprised when he'd offered it to her.

At the time she'd been offended and a little pissed off. But the more she thought about it, the more she realized he was right. They enjoyed having sex and hanging out, so why couldn't she stay with him after his mother left for Puerto Rico? Hell, she wasn't ready to walk away just yet either. Agreeing to extend their arrangement bought her some time to think about what she really wanted from Brandon, time to try to figure out what he wanted from her.

But she was pretty damn sure it wasn't a baby.

She blew her nose into her napkin.

Amara handed her a fresh one and waited until she was done cleaning herself up.

"Look, I get why you think Brandon isn't going to be around. But you need to make sure you don't push him away just because it will be harder for you if he decides he wants to be part of the baby's life. You really need to think carefully about this. And you know why."

Daisy didn't answer her. The lump in her throat wouldn't let her. She did know why, but she couldn't bring herself to say it.

Amara sighed and then squeezed her hand. "You of all people know what it's like to grow up believing that one of your parents didn't want you. And I know you'd never want to do that to your own child."

Amara was right. She would never do that to her own kid, especially if it wasn't true. She had to give Brandon the opportunity to be a part of this baby's life. If he chose not to, at least that would be on him and not her.

Her face crumpled, and this time she didn't bother hiding the tears.

"I'm sorry, honey. I shouldn't have said it that way," Amara rushed.

"No, you're right," she managed to squeak out.

"I hate that you're hurting so much right now. But I do

think you're making the right decision."

Daisy blew her nose on the last of the napkins. "I'll tell him tonight."

Amara's eyes widened. "Tonight? As in today's tonight?"

"Yeah, we're supposed to meet at Alexa's in a couple of hours to go out for one last dinner with Lorena before she leaves tomorrow. I'll tell him once we're home and—why do you have that strange look on our face."

Amara's eyes were shut and her nose was scrunched up as if she'd just taken a whiff of some bad cheese. She took a deep breath and then looked at Daisy.

"Let me just start by saying I had absolutely nothing to do with this."

Chapter Eighteen

I'm fine.

Brandon stared at the text Daisy had sent him an hour ago. He may not be an expert when it came to women, but he did know that "I'm fine" meant the exact opposite. So why wasn't Daisy fine?

Despite her initial hesitation to his proposal, she'd agreed to stay with him for another month. He had hoped she would've kept their arrangement more open-ended, but it seemed important to her to set a stop date.

She'd seemed back to normal the past few days. He replayed their morning in his head to see if he'd missed something. As usual, they'd reached for each other as soon as they were awake and they'd shared a long kiss good-bye before he left for the restaurant.

He'd texted her earlier in the day to ask how her appointment went and also if she wanted him to pick her up from the condo instead of taking separate cars to Alex's for their dinner. She'd only responded hours later that she'd meet him there.

So he'd asked if she was okay. The two-word text back gnawed at him.

Maybe he should call her.

"For someone who's about to open a third restaurant, you could try to look a little happier."

Brandon looked up from his phone to see Dante walking into his office. He stood up from his chair. "Are you saying what I think you're saying?"

"I am. It's all done. Everything has been approved. You, my friend, have just been given the official green light to start construction on Miami Cuchara."

Relief and excitement raced through his body. He went over and gave Dante a big bear hug. "*Gracias, amigo*."

"Don't thank me, thank Raphael. He had to do some major ass-kissing to get the planning commissioner back to the site in order to do a walkthrough before the city council vote last night. But you got the votes you needed and the project is a go. Speaking of, Raphael is ready to pull the trigger but he says he needs you over there as soon as possible before he can move forward with a few things. I told him you could probably fly out there this week. What do you say? Or do you have something else going on here that you need to wrap up before leaving for Miami?"

He let go of Dante. He knew his friend meant if there was anything holding him up this week. But it still made him think about what embarking on a new restaurant hundreds of miles away would mean to his life in the long term.

There were things that he'd have to put aside.

People he'd have to stop seeing so often.

Dante immediately noticed the change in his emotion. "What's wrong? I thought you'd be happier than this."

Brandon walked back to his desk and sat down. "I am happy. I guess I'm shocked is all. I didn't think it was ever going to happen. I even had Pilar call and tell the realtor over there to stop looking for condos."

"Well, tell her to start looking again. You have some time, Brandon. You could always move there later. Until then, you just do the back and forth like usual."

Usual meant living in hotels and eating in restaurants and not having ties to any city or anyone. Why did it suddenly seem so depressing?

"I guess. It's just that I was starting to get used to the idea of staying in L.A. for a little longer."

His friend took a seat. "And maybe you were also getting used to having someone around?"

Brandon rubbed his forehead. "My mom's leaving for Puerto Rico tomorrow and I told Daisy that I wanted to keep things going between us. So, yeah, I got used to the idea of having her around."

"Then stay in L.A.," Dante said as if it were really an option.

"What do you mean? This is my business. My livelihood. My brand. I have to move to Miami and make this restaurant a success."

"You just said it. The Cuchara restaurants are your business. They aren't *you*. And businesses are run every single day by people who don't own them. I'm not saying hand it over completely. I'm just saying that maybe it's time to start delegating some of that responsibility."

The thought of not being involved in every single decision from here until opening night never occurred to him. L.A. Cuchara had already been operational for nearly two years and he still was there every single day. The only reason he wasn't in New York as often was because it had been open for two years longer than L.A. Cuchara. That meant, eventually, L.A. Cuchara would get to the point where he could leave it totally to Alex. She'd already told him she was planning to stay put and had no desire to run the Miami kitchen once the restaurant opened.

Brandon saw no other choice. He hadn't worked this hard to fail. How could he risk the future of the Miami project on something that was never supposed to be forever?

"Running restaurants is who I am, Dante. And honestly, I don't know how to be anything else. Like you said last time, us Montoyas are no good at relationships. I'm good at making deals, and that's exactly what this thing with Daisy was. And now the deal is done. Simple as that."

"If you say so."

"I do. Believe me, it's better this way," he said and stood up. "I'll tell her tonight."

Dante, who had been slumped in his chair, straightened his back. "Tonight? Uh, don't you have a dinner or something to go to?"

"Yeah, with my mom and Alex. I was thinking I'd tell her afterward. Wait... How did you know about our dinner?"

His friend's dark complexion paled. "Uh, maybe you better sit back down for this."

Chapter Nineteen

Head down, Daisy dragged her feet up the driveway to Alexa's bungalow-style house. She carefully took each step as if she was plowing through mud instead of cobblestone.

"You're here." Brandon's voice made her look up. There he was. The father of her baby. He looked different. Or did he? Maybe it was just her pregnant imagination making her see things.

"I'm here," she said and tried to smile.

Brandon raised his eyebrow. "So you know?"

"I do. Amara told me. You?"

"Dante," he said, with a sheepish half grin. "I'm sorry."

She waved off his apology. "This isn't your fault. Who knew Alexa and your mom could pull off a surprise engagement party right under our noses?"

He nodded. "Well, almost a surprise. So, are you ready to go inside?"

Daisy looked at the house and then looked back at him. "No. But I will. Let's get this over with."

When Daisy was seven years old, she threw herself an

engagement party. She'd invited all of her stuffed animals and personally set out a feast of Oreo cookies, Pop Tarts, and Hawaiian Punch. And when the pretend guests started asking why her fiancé hadn't yet arrived to the party, she told them the truth—she didn't have a fiancé because she was never going to get married because she never wanted to end up like her parents: divorced. She just wanted to get dressed up and throw herself a party.

Today, though, she didn't even want the stupid party. Especially after she and Brandon walked through the door and were inundated with hugs and kisses and, well, love.

Daisy smiled through at all. If she didn't, she would cry.

She'd never felt so fake, so conniving. The genuine and heartfelt congratulations from her dad, Lorena, and others tugged at her conscience. She could feel the guilt rising in her throat like bile.

She spent the next hour swallowing that guilt and pretending she didn't hate herself as much as she did. It didn't help that Brandon kept disappearing, leaving her to answer questions about wedding dates and wedding locations and wedding dresses. The few times she did see him, he looked as miserable as she felt and she wondered how she'd ever get up the nerve to tell him her news.

"Daisy, have you had anything to eat?" Lorena pulled her away from a group of L.A. Cuchara employees who were trying to convince her to spill the secret details of Christian and Mira's upcoming wedding.

"Not yet. I'm not really hungry, though."

"You need to eat. Stay here and I'll go make you a plate."

She grabbed Lorena's arm. "That's not necessary. I can do it myself. Besides, I was going to go look for your son."

Lorena nodded and Daisy left her to chat with some guests who had just walked into the backyard. The thought of putting any food in her mouth made her stomach flip. But when she walked inside and saw her mother and stepfather standing in Alexa's foyer, the flip became more of a twist that became more of a knot.

She clenched her fists at her side and walked over to them. "Mom. Oliver. I didn't expect to see you here."

"Well, it was so last minute I almost didn't make it. But luckily I was able to cancel my other appointment," she said after pecking Daisy on the cheek.

"Congratulations, Daisy," her stepfather added stiffly and patted her shoulder.

"Thank you," she muttered.

"I have to say I'm a little surprised, Daisy. I would've thought this would've been a bigger celebration. With all of Brandon's celebrity customers and everything, I almost expected to see a red carpet on the driveway," her mother said as she surveyed the foyer and attached living room area, which was decorated boldly with black and white prints and splashes of the same ruby-red shade as Alexa's signature lipstick.

She should've known that it was the lure of attending a Hollywood party that made her mother make the trek out from Calabasas rather than the chance to celebrate her only daughter's engagement—fake or not.

"Well, I guess Brandon's mother and sister decided to keep it simple so we could celebrate with only our closest friends and family."

"How…sweet," she said.

"Can I get you guys something to drink?" Daisy asked before her mother could question anything else. She looked around for Brandon. Where the hell had he disappeared to? She needed a buffer. Quick.

Her stepfather answered for them both. "Sure, I'll take a beer and your mother will take a lemonade if you have it."

"I have no idea if we have it, but I'll go look. Why don't

you have a seat outside on the patio with the rest of the guests while I get those drinks?"

But her mother didn't budge. She folded her arms across her chest and planted her feet on the tile floor. "I'd like to meet my future son-in-law first, if you don't mind. Or am I going to have to wait until the day of the wedding?"

Daisy almost laughed. If that were the case then her mother would be waiting a very long time indeed. Then a glorious thought occurred to her. No actual wedding meant Daisy didn't have to worry about having to deal with her mother over guest lists, or menu options, or anything at all wedding-related. All she had to do was soldier through the next two hours and then it would be at least another few months until she'd be forced to talk to her mother again in order to tell her she was going to be a grandma.

Oh, God.

Daisy's moment of giddiness disappeared and real nausea threatened to spill her secret all over her mother's black Jimmy Choos.

"How about I go find Brandon and grab those drinks and meet you both on the patio?" She didn't wait for an answer, but instead walked briskly toward the kitchen.

As she turned the corner past the dining room, she saw Brandon and Pilar standing at the island counter. Brandon appeared to be looking through a pamphlet while Pilar stood next to him, her hand on his shoulder and her eyes focused on the side of his face. The way she looked at him sent bolts of uneasiness straight to Daisy's convulsing stomach.

"I can't wait until we leave," Pilar drawled. "I've always wanted to go to Miami."

The bolts intensified.

"It's a beautiful city," Brandon said while still looking at the pamphlet in his hands.

So, they were going to Miami. Huh. She didn't know what

bothered her more—the fact that he was going there with Pilar, or that he didn't tell her he was going at all. No wonder he wasn't kicking her out when his mother left tomorrow. He wasn't even going to be in town much longer anyway.

But he probably expects you'll still be here when he comes back, legs open and ready to welcome him home.

"I hear the hotel we're staying at has four different pools. And wait until you see the bikinis I found online—"

Daisy had heard enough. She stormed into the kitchen and walked right up to the island. "I, for one, would *love* to see your bikinis, Pilar. Oh, but I guess I'll have to wait, though, since apparently I'm not going to this amazing hotel with four pools."

Brandon's head shot up, and the smug look on Pilar's face sickened her. But it was the guilt on Brandon's that really made her want to hurl. She turned on her heel and headed for the bathroom, but Brandon caught her wrist before she could even leave the kitchen.

"Hey, it's not what you think. Let me explain." His voice was loud, but then dropped as he realized they had a patio full of guests just a few feet away.

"You don't have to explain anything to me," she replied, not caring about her volume.

"Maybe I don't have to, but I want to. Remember the Miami deal? I found out today that it's a go. Alex, Pilar, Dante, and I were thinking of flying to Miami next week to get the ball rolling. I'll only be gone a few days."

"That reminds me, guys," Pilar's stupid voice called out from the other side of the room. "I set up a meeting with your Miami realtor for Tuesday. Daisy, the realtor says she can email you the listings since you're not going to be there."

Daisy's heart fell. "A realtor?"

Brandon grabbed her hand and pulled her farther back into the kitchen. "Pilar, can you give us a moment, please?"

Pilar and her fake breasts sauntered out of the room, but not before giving Daisy her best, equally fake, smile. It was obvious the woman thought she knew something. Perhaps Daisy should've gone after her to get the truth, since Brandon wasn't going to give it up that easily.

"So now you're moving to Miami?"

"I don't know," he said, running his fingers over his short hair. "Maybe."

"When were you going to tell me?"

"Tonight, after the party. I literally just found out about this a few hours ago. Nothing is definite yet."

"But you have a realtor. So that means you're considering it."

"Of course I'm considering it. When we were building N.Y. Cuchara, I moved to an apartment just down the block so I could be there around the clock. When we were building L.A. Cuchara, I moved here for the same reason. So, yeah, that was the plan."

"Then why not tell me it was still a possibility? You said you thought the deal was dead."

"I thought it was."

"So me staying here with you was your backup plan? Until what? Until something, or someone, better and shinier came along?"

"I didn't say that."

"No. But since you're not saying anything else it means I'm right."

At that moment, the bile she'd been trying to push down ever since she'd walked in on Brandon and Pilar started to force its way back up. She covered her mouth and ran away from him, up the stairs and into Alexa's master bathroom.

Afterward, she gargled some mouthwash she'd found in the medicine cabinet and splashed cold water on her face. Looking into the mirror, she couldn't help but shake her head at her reflection.

Silly, silly girl. You knew this would happen eventually.

Deciding she couldn't do much more to fix herself up, she walked out of the bathroom half expecting to see Brandon waiting for her. Instead, she saw Lorena and immediately broke down into tears.

She pulled Daisy into an embrace, which only made her cry harder. Lorena ushered her to the bed to sit down and then left her to get tissues from the bathroom. Then she just let her cry on her shoulder until all that was left were strangled breaths.

"Do you want me to go downstairs and get you some club soda or some tea?" Lorena asked softly.

"No, thank you," Daisy mumbled. "Can we just sit here for a while?"

"We can sit here all night if you want. I told Brandon to let everyone know you weren't feeling well. They'll be gone soon. Your *papi* wanted to come say good-bye, but I told him that you would call him later."

"What about my mother?"

"Well, she didn't say too much. I think she already left, though. I'm so sorry I invited her. If I had known it would make you this upset, I would have never—"

"I'm not upset because of her. I'm upset because Brandon is moving to Miami."

"Oh, he's not moving there. He just told me that he's going over for a few days to get his new restaurant started. I guess he might go back and forth, but he can't move. You two have a wedding to plan and a baby to get ready for."

Daisy's head shot up and she looked at Lorena. "You know I'm pregnant? How?"

"A mother knows these things. You've been tired a lot and not eating the same things you used to eat. I followed you up here and, well, I heard you get sick. It all makes sense now. When did you find out?"

"This afternoon. I haven't had a chance yet to tell Brandon."

"Then tell him tonight and then tell him that you need him to be around more. Now that there's a baby coming, he can't be working so much."

"I can't tell him that, Lorena. I have no right to tell him that."

"Of course you do. You're going to be his wife."

Daisy took a deep breath and pulled away from Lorena. "No. No I'm not." And then she took Lorena's hands and finally told her the truth about everything.

When she was done, she offered her the box of tissues. "I'm so sorry for lying to you. You have to know that he only did this because he loves you and he was worried about you."

She braced herself for the woman's angry outburst or tears of betrayal. But there were neither. Instead, Lorena smiled and patted Daisy on the knee.

"*No te preocupes*. I won't kill him if that's what you're afraid of. I guess I think something was not right between you two when I first get here. But lately, I see things are different. He's different. And that's because of you. So I may not like that it happened this way, but how can I be mad or sad? I don't have the cancer anymore and I'm going to be an *abuela*."

Daisy smiled, but that didn't stop the tears from starting again. Lorena pulled her back in for a hug. "*Aye*, why are you crying again?"

"Because I can finally answer your question."

Lorena let go so Daisy could look at her. "Which question?"

"The one you asked me the first night you came here. You wanted to know when I knew that I was in your love with your son. I didn't have an answer back then because I was just pretending. But now…now I know."

"So tell me. Tell me when it was that you knew that you were in love with Brandon?"

"When I realized I could never force him to stay with me because of this baby. I love him too much to make him be something he doesn't want to be. He's going to Miami, Lorena. And I'm not going to stop him."

Lorena let out a big, long sigh. "I learned a long time ago that I need to let my son follow his own dreams. But I know him. He will do the right thing by you."

"And I'll do the right thing by him. I'll never keep this baby away from him. And I also promise that whatever happens between me and Brandon, you and Alexa will always be my family."

"Thank you...*mija*. Is it okay if I call you that now?"

"Yes." Daisy nodded furiously. "I would like that very much."

This time they both started crying.

Chapter Twenty

Brandon stood outside the bedroom door. He'd raised his hand to knock but stopped. Perhaps he should go back downstairs and give Daisy more time to calm down? He'd hated the way she'd looked at him when he told her he wasn't sure if he was moving to Miami. They should've talked about it more. She had every right to be pissed off.

Even his *mamá* was mad at him. She'd come into the kitchen after the last guest had left, slapped the back of his head, and told him to go upstairs and make things right with Daisy.

But as he stood there, his hand mid-knock, he realized he had no idea how to do that because he had no idea what Daisy wanted from him.

Guess it was time to find out.

He knocked lightly and she told him to come in. His heart sunk at the sight of her. It was obvious she'd been crying.

"Let's talk about this," he said as he walked toward her. "I'm sure we can—"

"I'm pregnant."

The words hit him like a knockout punch. The air wooshed out of his lungs, and he stumbled backward a few steps. She slowly lifted her head to meet his eyes then squared her shoulders. He knew she was challenging him to deny it was his. And perhaps if had it been any other woman, he would've.

But not Daisy. He knew in his heart that she was carrying his child. What he didn't know yet was how he felt about it.

"I'm sorry to tell you like this," she said after he still didn't respond. "I just found out at my doctor's appointment today and wanted to tell you tonight. But given everything that's happened... Well, I figured I couldn't leave without you knowing it."

"Are you..." He couldn't bring himself to ask the question. She nodded. "Yes, I'm keeping it."

Relief quickly replaced the shock. "Okay. Good. I'm glad."

"You're glad?" Her chin quivered and she hugged herself.

Glad wasn't the right word. He knew that. But what else could he say at the moment?

Just tell her what you're feeling.

That was the problem. He had no idea. "So now what?"

Disappointment shone in her eyes. Maybe he'd said the wrong thing?

"Well, first I'm going back to your house to start packing. The charade is over. I told your mom the truth about us."

More relief. "So that's what the slap in the head was for? Did you tell her about...?"

"She had already figured it out. She's happy, I think."

He smiled at the thought. "Of course she is. This is her dream come true."

"And you?" Her shoulders squared again.

He thought about the question. If he was being honest, he'd never considered the thought of being a father. Not because he hated the idea, but because he figured he'd be too busy doing other things with his life. Perhaps that was why he'd become a serial dater—preferring to spend his time with women who were as career-oriented as he was or too self-absorbed to even want to be a parent.

"Obviously, this isn't something I expected. I guess I'm going to need some time to get used to the idea."

Her gaze fell, and he knew she was disappointed with his answer again. He rushed to try to make it better. "You don't have to leave, Daisy. Stay so we can figure things out."

"Brandon—"

"Look, I know this isn't how we planned for things to happen, but it's happening. So why don't we make the best of it? I don't have to move to Miami. You and the baby can move in with me and—"

"And what? We can pretend to be a family like we were pretending to be engaged? I'm tired of pretending, Brandon. I just want to go home—my home. Besides, me being pregnant doesn't mean you have to change your plans. I'm perfectly capable of doing this on my own."

Why did she always want to prove how independent she was? This wasn't about helping her with a referral. This was about a baby, their baby.

"I'm not doubting that. All I'm saying is that you don't have to. I grew up without a dad and it sucked. I want to be a part of this baby's life."

"And you will be, I promise," she said. "But just because we're having a baby together doesn't mean we have to live together."

"Why not?"

"Because you don't love me. And if I stayed anyway, knowing that, then I'd probably resent you for not being around and sooner or later you'd resent me, too. I may screw up this mom thing eventually, but even I know that a baby deserves more than parents who can't stand each other."

His gut twisted at the obvious pain in her eyes. He wanted

to reassure her, take that hurt away. "I'd never resent you, Daisy."

"You don't know that." She shook her head and sat on the edge of the bed. "Look, I understand you need to be free to come and go as you want, and I don't want to be the reason you have to think twice about working all night or taking off across the country just because of some distorted sense of obligation or responsibility. I'm not your mother or your sister. You don't have to give up everything to stay with me."

"So I can be in the baby's life, but I can't be in yours?"

"Not if you're only going to be in it because you think that's what you're supposed to do. Go to Miami, Brandon. Move there if you want. It doesn't really matter to me anymore."

Irritation bubbled within him. Why was she being so cold? He was trying to do the right thing and all she could do was bring up Miami. "I already told you that I'm only going to be gone for a few days…or a week tops."

"And then what? You're going to leave again a few weeks after that? What if I'm due around the same time the restaurant is going to open? Then what?"

Frustration had tightened every muscle, every tendon. Finally, he snapped. "I don't know, okay! This deal has been in the works before I even asked you to be my pretend fiancée! Obviously I had no idea there'd be a baby to consider after all of this. So what am I supposed to do?"

"As usual, you're missing the point." She stood up then. Her eyes burned with anger instead of sadness. It had been a while since she'd looked at him like that. "I'm not asking you to do anything, okay? You don't have to choose between being eligible bachelor Brandon Montoya or being a father to this baby. And you don't have to be a husband, either. Happy now?"

"Daisy, I didn't mean—" He shouldn't have raised his voice at her, but he was just so damn confused. And pissed.

She'd dropped this bomb on him and then basically asked him to make decisions about the rest of his life right there on the spot. He couldn't do that. He wouldn't do that. His head throbbed with frustration.

"I'll let you know how things are going, and if you want to be there when the baby is born, of course I'll let you. If you decide later you want to work out some type of visitation arrangement, have Dante call me. Oh, and just so you know, I'm going to keep in touch with Lorena and Alexa. It's not their fault we couldn't work things out, right?"

He watched her pull the Tiffany engagement ring off her finger. She held it out in front of him.

"I told you that was yours," he said, shaking his head.

"It was never mine. We both know that."

When he still didn't take the ring, she shrugged and walked over to Alexa's dresser in the corner and set it down. Then she walked out of the room.

He knew the conversation was over. For now. They both needed time to think about things, and, so he wouldn't snap again, he sat on his sister's bed and waited until he heard her car leave. Then he headed back downstairs.

Luckily, his mother and Alex were nowhere to be found, because he really wasn't in the mood to answer their questions. So he grabbed his keys, got into his car, and started driving. As he navigated the winding roads leading up into the Santa Monica Mountains, Brandon replayed his conversation with Daisy over and over in his head and still couldn't quite understand what in the hell had just happened.

Because you don't love me.

Her words had sounded like an accusation. Still, she hadn't said she loved him, either.

Would it have made a difference?

As he continued to drive, he thought about the question. There was no doubt in his mind that he'd grown to care for her. How could he not? She was sexy and funny and had taken care of his *mamá* as if she was really her family. He missed her when she wasn't with him and relished every moment when he was. Daisy had become an important part of his life. And now she was going to have a baby. His baby.

Holy shit. He was going to be a dad.

His mouth grew dry and he gripped the steering wheel until his knuckles turned white. How on earth could he be a dad when he was just about to dive into a new restaurant project? If his schedule was crazy now, it was only going to get crazier. There were no ifs, ands, or buts about it. That's how it had to be for a project of this magnitude. And he owed it to himself and everyone else who had already worked so hard to make it happen to do whatever it took to ensure this restaurant was as successful as his others.

Daisy had told him that he didn't have to change his life because of the baby. Maybe not. But the more he thought about it, the more he wanted to. This project was going to take all of his time and energy but he would dig deep to find more for this baby.

Perhaps if she had shown any hint at all that she cared about him the way he cared about her, he could've found a way to make it work between them, too. After all, they enjoyed being with each other in and out of bed. Why couldn't that be enough?

She kept talking about him moving to Miami as if he was the one abandoning her. But she was the one who seemed ready and willing to leave once there was no more reason to pretend to be engaged. If that's what she really wanted, then he wasn't going to try to stop her.

Instead, he was going to focus on building his new restaurant and getting ready for the baby.

He was going to be a dad.

This time, the thought didn't freak him the hell out.

Chapter Twenty-One

It was true that Daisy had only planned one other wedding. But even she knew it was a bad sign when the bride was late to her own rehearsal dinner.

That's why she couldn't lie to Christian when he asked her for the third time if Mira had called.

"No, I'm sorry. But that doesn't mean that she isn't going to walk through that door right now."

They both looked toward the entrance to the winery. And as hard as she willed the doors to open, they stayed closed. "Listen, why don't you go sit down, or have a drink and mingle? I'll go wait outside for her, okay?"

The worry in his eyes when he looked at her nearly broke her heart. Although Mira had become a good friend, Daisy cursed her at that moment. As she walked outside, she replayed last night's phone conversation between them. She'd seemed off, distracted almost. When Daisy pressed, though, she'd insisted everything was fine. Then before they hung up, Daisy had made a joke about reselling everything she'd purchased after the wedding.

Mira had laughed about it, but then said: "And, hey, if I became one of those runaway brides, you could probably get twice the money, right?"

Although the comment had nagged at her, Daisy brushed it off.

Because you were more worried about table place cards than your friend.

Resigned to the fact that she was probably the worst wedding planner ever, she began walking down the winery's long driveway. Cars lined each side. According to her last check of the guest list, nearly everyone had showed. Everyone, that is, except for the bride.

Daisy pulled out her phone to check for messages one last time. There were none. She was just about to shove the phone back into her pocket when it vibrated and played the ringtone version of "Here Comes The Bride."

"Oh my God, Mira. Are you okay? Where the hell are you?"

"I'm in the backseat of my car."

"Excuse me? Are you hurt or sick? Should I get Christian so we can come get you."

"No. Don't get Christian. You come here first. I'm two cars down."

"What do you mean?"

"I'm here, Daisy. At the winery. My car is parked just a few feet away from you. The doors are unlocked." The line clicked.

Daisy looked up and surveyed the line of cars again. She took a few steps and then she saw Mira's silver Mercedes. Peeking inside, she saw her friend lying down in the backseat. Daisy opened the front passenger door and slid in.

"Why haven't you come inside yet?" she asked without turning around. "Christian is starting to freak out. And quite frankly, I'm in the middle of a panic attack."

"I don't know, Daisy," Mira said. "I don't know. I got here at four, like I was supposed to. But then I couldn't get out of the car so I turned back around and left. I've been driving for the past hour or more. I couldn't figure out where to go so I came back here and parked. I didn't want anyone to see me so I've been hiding out here in the back."

"What's going on with you, Mira? Are you having second thoughts about marrying Christian?"

"I love Christian. I'm absolutely sure of that."

"And he loves you. You know that, right?"

"I do. But maybe it's not enough. Maybe we're just too different to make this marriage thing work out."

"Or maybe this marriage is going to last forever *because* you are so different."

"What about you and Brandon? You told me you thought you guys came from different worlds and that's why you broke up."

It had been nearly three weeks since Daisy had moved out of Brandon's condo and back into her apartment. They'd been the hardest three weeks of her life. Her morning sickness was in full effect, which made wedding errands more difficult. She'd finally confessed everything to Mira, and fortunately she hadn't fired her on the spot. They'd had a long talk over virgin margaritas, and Mira forgave her. Whether it had more to do with the fact that she hadn't wanted to make a pregnant woman cry than really understanding why she'd lied, it didn't even matter. All that mattered was getting the wedding over with so she could focus on getting her life back on track with or without Brandon.

She hadn't really talked to him since the day he left for Miami. She knew she had to eventually. She had a doctor's appointment the next day, and she'd promised when he left that she'd keep him informed. He'd wanted to fly back for the appointment, but she told him it wasn't necessary and he didn't argue with her. It seemed like a hundred years ago that the only thing the two of them could do together was argue.

And for a brief wisp of a second, she missed that.

She used to tell herself that Brandon pushed her buttons because he was so different from her. But she'd come to realize that he pushed those buttons for other reasons altogether.

"Is that what this is about?" she asked, still looking straight ahead. "Me and Brandon?"

Her friend sighed. "No, it's about me and Christian. But you have to admit, the circumstances are similar.

"Look, Mira. Brandon and I didn't work out because our relationship was fake. We were only pretending to be a couple. How can you have a future with someone when your past is a lie? What you and Christian have is real. You have to know that. Otherwise you would never have said yes."

"I'm scared, Daisy."

"Of course you are. I'd think you're crazy if you weren't scared. Although to clarify, I think hanging out in the parking lot while your rehearsal dinner is going on is a little wacko, too."

Mira laughed. "I'm so glad I stole a beer for you."

"Me, too," Daisy said and finally exhaled. "So, does that mean you're ready to go inside?"

"Yes."

"Are you sure? Because, seriously, Mira, if you don't want to marry Christian then just say the word, and I'll jump behind the wheel and drive us anywhere you want to go."

A hand reached between the seats and grabbed hers. "Thank you. But I'm good. I love him and I want to marry him."

"Awesome. Then let's go."

Mira sat up and they exited the car together. Once they were both standing, she grabbed Daisy and gave her a hug. "You're a good friend," she said.

"I know. Now, let me go and be an even better wedding planner." Daisy started to walk away, but Mira wouldn't let her go. "What's wrong now?"

"Christian says Brandon is miserable in Miami. But he doesn't want to talk about it. Or you."

Daisy shrugged. "I can't help what he does or doesn't want to talk about. I'm not his fiancée anymore."

"That doesn't mean you don't love him anymore."

"I never said that I did."

"Maybe that's why he went to Miami."

"Nope. Brandon went to Miami because he wanted to go to Miami. That's what he does. That's who he is. I've always known he'd never change."

"Did you ever ask him to?" Mira let her go finally and they started back to the winery.

"Damn brides," Daisy muttered. "They always think they know everything."

· · ·

Two days later she pushed thoughts of Brandon out of her mind and focused on finishing her *To Do* list for the wedding. In between errands, she stopped at her dad's house to deliver a spare suitcase.

She had no idea she'd be treated to an impromptu fashion show as well.

"Well, what do you think?" her dad asked and spun around in front of her.

Could she think? Her fifty-seven-year-old dad was standing before her dressed in Bermuda shorts and a Hawaiian shirt. In all her years of living, she'd never seen her dad's legs or his knees. Old soccer injuries and multiple surgeries had mangled them enough that he'd always told her it was better for everyone if he kept them hidden away underneath his work pants, jeans, or his church slacks. It turned out that despite the assorted bumpy scars and chicken-like appearance, his legs weren't that bad.

God, did she just really check out her dad's legs?

After she shook that disturbing thought out of her head, Daisy found her way to the couch and sat down.

"I know it's not what I usually wear but Teresa says that this is what all the men wear on these cruises. I have two more outfits just like this, but in different colors," her dad said with a wink.

And that's when she saw him—really saw how different he was, and it had nothing to do with his new clothes or his willingness to show off legs like a Rockette. Her dad was happy with Teresa. How could she not be happy for him?

She got up and gave him a hug. "You look great," she said while resting her chin on his shoulder.

"Thank you, *mija*. Even if you're lying through your teeth, thank you. Okay, are you hungry? I can warm up some *pozole* that Teresa made last night?"

Seeing her dad beaming like a teenager had lifted her spirits and inspired her appetite. "*Pozole* sounds good. But aren't you going to go change again? You leave for your cruise tomorrow and you don't want to spill anything on your new clothes, do you?"

He agreed and within a few minutes he was back in his usual jeans and soccer jersey and sat down with her at the table to eat. They chatted some more about his upcoming cruise to Ensenada. It was only for three days but it might as well have been for an entire month the way he described everything he and Teresa were planning to do.

"I'm really glad Teresa talked you into taking this trip. I can't even remember the last time you went on a vacation."

"Me either," he said with a laugh. "We're both disappointed we're going to miss Mira's wedding tomorrow

She's a nice girl. I'm glad she's your friend."

"Me, too."

Her dad nodded his head. They ate quietly for a few minutes, and she allowed herself to enjoy the smoky and delicious stew made with pieces of pork and hominy. The deep red broth soothed her throat but also offered a kick with the combination of spices—dried chiles, oregano, onions and garlic. She'd been savoring the soup so deeply that her dad's voice startled her from out of the blue, "So have you told your mother about the baby yet?"

She swallowed hard, the *pozole* burning her throat on the way down. "Nope. I was hoping to wait until he or she graduated from college before having to break the news."

"Daisy…"

"What? You were married to the woman. How do you think she's going to react to the news that she's going to be a grandma? She had a hissy fit last year when her travel agent asked if she qualified for the airline's senior discount."

Her dad laughed and then his eyes widened. "I just remembered the last time I went on a vacation. I think you were three or four and we drove to San Francisco to visit your mother's aunt. It took us about four hours longer than normal because your mother kept making me pull over to the side of the road."

"Really? I don't even remember that."

"Well, it was a long time ago. After the driving part was all over, it actually turned out to be a very nice trip. We had a good time there. Even your mother."

It was hard to picture her mother like that. In fact, it was hard to picture the three of them doing something together as a family. For so long it had been just her and her dad. Her mother didn't belong in that picture.

Had she ever?

She took a breath and blurted out, "Why did you ever

marry her?" He stopped sipping his soup, then wiped his mouth with a napkin and looked at her. Immediately she regretted the question. "I'm sorry. I shouldn't have asked that."

Her dad reached over and patted her hand. "It's okay, *mija*. It's okay to talk about her. I know it's been hard for you and I'm sure you had lots of questions, but you never asked them. So ask now."

Where to start? She wanted to know so much. She wanted to know why her mother left them and whether he'd tried to stop her. She wanted to know how he could make Daisy go to her mother's new husband's house and pretend that she didn't hate her, didn't despise her. She wanted to know all those things, but she just asked him the same question as before.

"Why did you ever marry her?"

He sighed as he looked around the kitchen. "She was a different person before we got married. Besides being beautiful, she was smart. Much smarter than me. Funny, back then I always used to be afraid that one day she'd figure out she could do better and break up with me. I just never thought she'd do it after we were married, or after we had a baby."

His hand gripped hers and she looked away before he could see the tears she knew brimmed her eyes. "I never wanted you to know this, but maybe you should so you can finally realize that she didn't leave because you weren't a good enough daughter."

One tear finally escaped—just like her secret.

Her father continued. "Even though you never said it, I knew that's what you thought back then. And I know that's what you still think. But you're wrong. Your mother was never cut out to be a mother. She left because she knew that you deserved better than what she could ever give you."

Daisy wiped away the tear. "Sorry, Dad, but that's crap. That's just the excuse she uses because she feels guilty for leaving us."

"It's not crap, Daisy. Your mother told me she didn't want kids even before we got married."

The words shook her. "She actually said that to you?"

"She did. Many times. But I was young and in love, and I thought that once we were married she'd change her mind. You have to remember, it was a different time back then. I'd never heard of a woman who didn't want to be a mother. I thought those feelings would go away. But they didn't."

"Then why did you have me?"

"We'd been married for seven years already and I guess she was tired of me asking, of her mother asking, of her *abuelita* asking. So one day I come home from work and she's not home. There's no dinner waiting for me, no note. Nothing. I call everyone we know and nobody has seen her all day. Finally, around eight o'clock or something, she comes walking through the door with a suitcase. She'd taken a bus all the way to Santa Barbara, but when she got there she realized she didn't know what to do next. So she got back on the bus and came home to me."

"What did you do?"

"That night, I didn't do anything. But the next day, I came home early from work and we sat down and talked. She said she wanted to get a job and I said I wanted to have a baby. So we talked about it some more and she agreed to have a baby as long as she could get a job when you started school. And that's what happened. Your first day of kindergarten she found a part-time job working at the appliance store and, well..."

And two years later, her mother left her father for the owner's son and became the store's manager. The only thing she took from their marriage was a set of dishes. She'd left everything else—including Daisy—with her ex-husband.

"I know you blame your mother for a lot of things, *mija*. But it was my fault, too."

"How can you even say that, Dad?"

"Because I pushed her to be a mother. She always thought she was meant for a different life than the one I gave her. I think it ate at her every day. Of course she was miserable here."

"Fine. Maybe I can kind of see why she needed to leave in the first place. But that doesn't make up for how she was when I was older. How she still is."

"You have to accept that you and her are never going to have a real mother and daughter relationship. But she's still your blood, and maybe you can have a different kind of relationship. And, one day, I hope you can finally forgive her. I have."

"You have?"

"It took me a long time, *mija*. A very long time. Maybe if I could've forgiven her sooner, then I could've been a better father to you."

She opened her mouth to argue, but he held up his hand so he could finish talking. "I loved you so much, but I didn't know what to do with you. So I worked and made sure that I could buy you things and send you to college. I thought your *tias* could help with the other stuff but I know now I should've been around more."

"It wasn't that bad."

"Maybe. But I know it could've been better."

"I can't believe you're not angry at her anymore."

"How can I be angry at someone who gave me the greatest joy in my life…you."

Her tears fell freely now, and Daisy wiped them away with a laugh. "Geeze, Dad. Now my *pozole* is going to be salty from all these tears."

"Just add some more lemon and it will be perfect again."

They hugged and then went back to eating. "I guess I can call her next week then," she said softly.

"Whenever you're ready." He paused for a few seconds. "What about Brandon?"

That had been her dad's first question, too, when she'd told him about the baby. She'd cried, of course. And perhaps her tears had been the reason why he hadn't exploded when she also told him about the fake engagement. But she would've welcomed that reaction instead of the deafening silence he put her through for the next two days. It had been Teresa, apparently, who'd finally made him call her so they could talk about things. She knew she'd hurt him with her deception.

It had taken some time to get back to being like this with each other again. The mention of Brandon, though, made her worry that the conversation was going to take a very different turn.

She paused before answering her dad's question. "What about him? I talked to him last night to tell him about my doctor's appointment."

"No, I mean when are you going to stop being angry at Brandon."

"Have *you* stopped being angry at Brandon?"

Her dad sighed. "I was angry when I thought he'd abandoned you. But now that I know he's planning to take care of this baby, I'm not angry anymore. And you?"

She moved her spoon around the bowl. "I'm not angry at Brandon either."

He sighed again. "Your face gets red and your body stiffens whenever you say his name. You're not a little girl anymore, Daisy. It's time to stop playing these games."

Daisy finally looked up at her dad. "What games?"

"The games where you pretend you don't have feelings for him. Maybe you weren't really going to get married, but I know you. And I could see that you cared about him, and I could see he cared about you."

"Maybe that's true. But whatever we had, it wasn't enough. It's too late."

"*Basta!* It's never too late if you love someone. You need

to tell him what you're feeling and then forgive him."

"Forgive him for being who he's always been? He didn't promise me anything, and he sure didn't expect this," she said, pointing to her stomach. "You just told me how miserable mom was because you forced her to have me. Why would I want to do the same thing to him and my baby?"

"Brandon and your mother are two different people. You know Brandon wants to be a father. He's already proving it. I'm not saying I want you to force him into anything."

"Then what are you saying?"

"I'm saying it's time to be honest with him about how *you* feel about *him*. You're angry because he left. But did you give him a reason, besides the baby, to stay? You need to tell him that you're in love with him, *mija*."

She winced in surprise. "Did you talk to Mira or something?"

"No, why?"

"Because she said the same thing."

"See, I knew I liked her. It's the truth, right?"

She nodded just as her eyes watered with another round of tears. "I'm scared, Daddy. I'm scared that he'll never love me the way that I love him. He's this beautiful, rich, successful man who has been all over the world and parties with movie stars and models. He has this exciting and amazing life. Why would he ever choose me over that?"

"*Aye, mija*. You don't give yourself, or him, enough credit. Love is more than all of those things. You're scared now, but think of how you'll feel if you never tell him—if you don't fight for what you want. I may not have taught you things when you were a little girl, but I want you to learn from me now. I've lived my life full of regret and it's made me miss out on so much. Please, *mija*, don't be like me."

Chapter Twenty-Two

"Alex!"

Brandon stalked through the dilapidated building searching for his sister, kicking up dust and scraps of trash along the way.

"Alex!" Anger burned through him, heating his blood and making every muscle tighten until it ached. He'd been in Miami for nearly three weeks now, and everything that could go wrong with the project had. The cost to renovate the building seemed to double every day due to the number of problems his project manager kept discovering. He'd had enough.

"Alex!"

"What!" His sister came running inside and met him in the kitchen area.

"I've been looking all over you. Where were you?"

"I had to make a phone call and the signal is better outside. What's wrong?"

"I fired Raphael."

"What? Are you freaking crazy? He's been working on

this project for you for months. What happened?"

What *didn't* happen would probably be the better question. Would anything ever go right on this project?

"He just told me that I may have to rethink my idea about a water fountain in the front because they dug up some of the patio tiles and realized the electrical access isn't as clear cut as the original blueprints showed."

Alexa shrugged. "So? It's not his fault if the old blueprints are, you know, old. That's no reason to fire him."

"I didn't fire him for that. I fired him because he told me that he quit."

His sister's eyes widened and her mouth dropped. "Oh my God, Brandon. What did you do?"

Why did she automatically think he'd done something wrong?

"Nothing. I just told him that I was pissed off about these new problems and that he should've figured all of this out before I spent so much money buying this shitty building."

"And?"

"And I told him that if one more thing went wrong, I'd make sure he'd never work on a restaurant project in this town again. So he called me an asshole and told me he quit. So I said he couldn't quit because he was fired."

Alex shook her head and sighed. "Dammit, Brandon. You need to fix this. Do you know how long it's going to take to find a new project manager and construction company and get them up to speed on everything that needs to happen by our first inspection?"

"Then we delay the opening—or we don't open at all."

"What do you mean?"

"I mean that maybe it's not worth it. This building is a mess, and I just don't know if it's worth all of the additional money it's going to take to get it to where it should be. So maybe I should cut my losses now, sell the fucking thing, and go back to L.A."

Alex nodded as if she knew something he didn't. "Let me guess. This is because you talked to Daisy yesterday."

The mention of Daisy twisted his muscles into a tighter knot. "What does that have to do with anything?"

"It has everything to do with this. You've been kind of a jerk since we got here, but you've been an absolute monster since that phone call. What happened?"

He pulled a folding chair over from the corner and sat down. The magnitude of his argument with Raphael and everything else that had happened over the past few days weighed him down. He rubbed his eyes and then put his head in hands.

The sound of another chair being dragged across the cracked linoleum made his head hurt even more. Then he felt a hand on his shoulder.

"Tell me, Brandon. What happened with Daisy?" his sister asked softly.

He shrugged. "I don't know what happened with Daisy. That's the problem."

"What did she tell you?"

"Not much. She had her appointment yesterday with her new doctor. Her regular doctor had told her that she was going to be retiring before the baby was born so she referred her to someone else. Daisy says she likes the new doctor and that everything is fine and that she goes back next month."

"Oh. Well, that's good. I don't understand then. What's wrong? And don't tell me nothing's wrong because since we've been in Miami, you've fired Pilar, the interior decorator, me a few times, and now Raphael."

"I don't know how to explain it. The last time I talked to Daisy back in L.A., it was weird, like we were polite strangers. And it was the same yesterday."

There was an uncomfortableness between them now, and

it was obvious that both were choosing their words carefully.

He looked at his sister. "And that's not us, Alex. I just wish I could fix it so things could go back to how they were before."

"You can't go back. After everything that's happened, you're not the same person you were before, and neither is she."

"Well, she's definitely not the same. But I don't think I've changed."

"Are you kidding me? You used to love every single little thing that went into opening a new restaurant. Now, it's like you hate it. Like it's something you *have* to do, not something you *want* to do. And the old Brandon would've already rented a place here in Miami. Instead you're living out of a suitcase at a hotel. Why? Because Miami isn't your home and I don't think you ever want it to be your home."

He laughed bitterly. "I thought you knew better, little sister. I'm Brandon Montoya. My home is wherever my restaurant is."

Alex patted him on the back and gave him a slight smirk. "Not anymore, big brother. We both know that your home is back in L.A. with Daisy and your baby."

He stood up and walked around the dark and dank kitchen. As he studied the grease-covered walls and curtains of cobwebs, he realized Alex was right. He hated this place. But not because it looked like a disaster. For all his ranting and raving, he knew there was potential underneath. No, he hated it because he knew that Daisy would probably never even set foot in it.

He turned to face his sister and covered his gaping mouth with one hand. No wonder he'd been such an asshole in Miami. The project wasn't the one falling apart. He was.

Brandon raised his arms, clasped his hands together, and dropped them on top of his head. Then he closed his eyes and let out a deep breath.

"I think I love her, Alex," he announced.

"You think?"

"Well, I've never been in love before. How do I know for sure?"

She spit out a laugh. "Don't ask me. Given the number of boyfriends I've kicked to the curb in the past year, it's obvious I don't know either. You know there's only person in our family who can help you figure this out, right?"

He nodded. His *mamá* had always said that she loved their father from the moment she first met him. And even though he'd been gone for more than twenty years, that love hadn't dimmed one bit. His heart hurt thinking about the deep anguish she must live with every day because their father wasn't with her.

He'd never understood that anguish until now. It was exactly how he'd been feeling ever since Daisy had left him.

Brandon realized he didn't need to ask his *mamá* how he could figure out if he really loved Daisy. He already knew.

And that made his head hurt all over again. Things between them had gone to shit. He couldn't just show up and tell her what he'd discovered. Based on who he was and how he'd lived until this moment, she'd never believe him.

Brandon went back to the chair and sat down. "What am I going to do, Alex? How do I make things right? I know Daisy. She's going to think I want to be with her only because she's pregnant. How can I convince her it's more than that?"

"Like I said before, I'm definitely not the expert when it comes to things like this. But I've gotten to know Daisy over the past year, and it seems to me that she's not the kind of girl who needs big showy declarations of feelings. The more meaningful and from the heart, the better."

"So, do the exact opposite of what I think I should do?"

"Yeah, pretty much." When he groaned, she threw one arm around his shoulder. "Seriously, Brandon. If you love her like we both think you do, deep down you'll know how to tell her."

That may be so. But what he didn't tell Alex was how fucking scared he was when he thought about the many different things she might tell him back.

Chapter Twenty-Three

Christian Santos and Mira Alvarez were married at sunset underneath a white canopy on the grounds of the Downtown Los Angeles Public Library. It was a beautiful and intimate ceremony attended by only about fifty of their closest friends and family.

Luckily, tabloid reporters and paparazzi missed the entire thing, since multiple anonymous tips had falsely led them to the backyard of a Malibu beach house, which coincidentally *also* had a white canopy and about fifty people standing around it.

As Daisy helped event staff untie floral displays from around the tent, she smiled to herself.

She'd done it. She'd pulled off a major celebrity wedding in only a few weeks. That had to be a record in Hollywood. Even more important, though, were the looks on Christian's and Mira's faces when they hugged her before they left to take photos inside the historic building. They thanked her over and over again for giving them the perfect wedding, and that's why she couldn't stop smiling. Or crying.

God, she was a hormonal mess.

Daisy wiped her eyes and untied the last floral display. She arranged it in a box with the others and asked one of her helpers to take it to the reception area. But just as she was about to tell him to be careful and not smash the arrangements, Brandon walked through the wall of sheer fabric draped at the tent's entrance.

Her breath stuttered.

He was dressed in the suit he'd worn when he took her to that Italian restaurant. Not only did it fit him perfectly, but it enhanced his dark eyes and dark hair in a way that triggered all kinds of lust-filled urges. But this was neither the time nor the place to think about that. So she shook a little to wake herself up and waited for him to approach her.

"It was a beautiful wedding," he said when he did.

His words threw her off. Why hadn't she seen him before now? "I didn't even know you were here."

"I know. I kind of hid in the back. I figured you had a lot to do and I didn't want to distract you."

"Distract me? Wow. Aren't you the confident one?" The remark came out without her even thinking about it. He laughed and she allowed herself to join him. It felt nice, actually. When was the last time they had done such a simple thing together?

"I miss your laugh," he said, reading her mind.

That quieted her. Just like that, they were back to being wary of each other. Her throat tightened, and she silently pleaded with herself to keep her crazy emotions in check.

"Do Christian and Mira know you're here? I'm sure they were wondering if you'd show up."

"Why wouldn't I show up? They're my friends and…and I knew you'd be here."

"Brandon." She choked on his name thanks to the painful lump in her throat.

"What?"

"I know we have to talk, but I need to make sure everything is ready inside."

She started to walk away but he stepped in front of her. "Wait. I need to give you something." He held out a blue Tiffany's bag that she hadn't noticed before.

Her heart pounded and she took a step backward. If this was a joke, it was a dumb one. "I hope that's a gift for the bride and groom."

He didn't answer. Instead, he set the bag on the ground and pulled out a small, white box. Daisy held her breath as he lifted the lid. She expected to see the Tiffany engagement ring she'd left behind. But she didn't.

Brandon took the ring out of the box and showed it to her. It was a silver filigree band with one small diamond in the center and even smaller turquoise pieces set on each side. It was simple, yet elegant. It was perfect.

"I flew to Puerto Rico last night because I wanted to ask my *mamá* for this. It was my *abuelita's*. She never had a real wedding ring, but supposedly my grandfather bought this for her when she became pregnant with my mother."

She shook her head wildly. "I can't accept it, Brandon. It should go to Alexa. I don't need a ring. I thought I made myself clear about that."

"First of all, Alexa also wants you to have it. Second of all, I'm not giving this to you just because you're pregnant. I'm giving it to you because, dammit, I love you, Daisy."

Her body betrayed her yet again, and tears fell from the corners of her eyes. "Since when?"

"Since I realized that being with you is more satisfying than opening ten restaurants. That talking to you and laughing with you is more fun than going to a hundred movie premieres or club openings. And that making love to you is more thrilling and breathtaking than anything else I've ever done in my life. I'm hoping you feel the same way. Please tell me you feel the same way."

The pounding of her heart hit epic proportions. "Stay here. I have something to show you." She could see his disappointment in the way his face fell, so she ran to the corner of the tent and retrieved her purse from underneath one of the covered tables. She ran back to him, grabbed the manila envelope from her purse, and handed it to him.

He arched his eyebrow and pulled out the white paper that was inside, still holding tight to the ring. "What is this? I don't understand," he said as he scanned the paper.

"It's a one-way ticket to Miami. I was going to take a red-eye flight after the reception and surprise you at your hotel."

Brandon looked up at her. His eyes shone with emotion and it filled her heart. "But you said you'd never fly."

"I know. And I'm pregnant so I wouldn't be able to take anything either—I'd have to fly stone cold sober. But I was going to do it because the only thing scarier to me than getting on that plane was trying to make it through one more day without you. I love you, Brandon, and I want to be with you."

He dropped the paper and the envelope and went to her. When his lips crushed hers, she whimpered. It was such an exquisite relief to be able to taste him again. Now she understood what he had meant when he said Puerto Rico would always be his mother's *asopao*. For her, love would always be the taste of him.

When they finally broke for air, she sighed in pleasure.

"I love you," he said looking into her eyes. "I need you. *Usted puede ser mi salvación*."

"And what would I be saving you from?"

"A life without you," he said and got down on one knee. "Marry me, Daisy. For real."

Tears blurred the sight before her, but it still took her breath away. "Yes," she cried and nodded. "Yes, I'll marry you."

He slid the ring on her finger and then stood up and cupped her face with his hands. "Are you sure?"

She nodded and he kissed her again, then he pressed his forehead against hers. "I can't believe this is really happening."

"Me either. Who would've ever thought that we'd end up together?"

He moved his hands from her face down to her waist and pulled her against him. "And only we would get engaged, get pregnant, break up, and then get married," he said chuckling.

"Hey, it's not my fault you couldn't see what was right in front you," she said, trying to sound offended.

Brandon pulled back to look at her. "Me? What about you? If I remember correctly, you were the one pretending you didn't want to sleep with me that night after Amara's wedding. Which brings me to the second thing I brought for you."

Daisy couldn't imagine what it could be. So when he reached inside his jacket pocket and pulled out a familiar looking hotel key card, she laughed.

"Don't tell me…"

"I booked the honeymoon suite at the Esperanza for the rest of the weekend. I figured since we were doing things out of order anyway…"

She laughed again until a thought occurred to her. "What if I had said no," she asked.

"I also booked it for next weekend and the weekend after that and the weekend after that. Let's just say I was prepared in case it took me a while to convince you that we belong together."

Her heart filled with pure joy. "Now, how could I argue with that?"

He shrugged. "You can't. But don't worry. We've got the rest of our lives to argue about silly things like who loves who more."

"Well, I already know the answer to that one. It's—"

Brandon kissed her before she could finish her sentence, and she didn't protest one bit. If this was the way they ended all disagreements from here on out, she couldn't wait for the next one.

Acknowledgments

To my editor Heather Howland for your lessons in conflict and motivation and for always challenging me to dig deeper.

To Kim at Read Your Writes Book Reviews for hating the idea of Brandon and Daisy as a couple so much that it motivated me to work harder to make their story more believable. I hope I've convinced you that they belong together. :)

To my friends in OCC RWA and Facebook Night Writers for your continuing support.

To my best beta reader Valentine Greiner for your genuine excitement and love of my stories.

To Louisa Bacio, Nikki Prince and Elizabeth Scott for our late night write-ins that actually get some writing and editing accomplished in between the laughing and many glasses of wine.

To my family for their unwavering support and unconditional love.

To my auntie Elva for being willing to answer my questions about your diagnosis and treatment and, especially, for being a one-year cervical cancer survivor.

To my husband Patrick and our kids, thank you for it all. I love you.

About the Author

Sabrina Sol is the chica who loves love. She writes steamy romance stories featuring smart and sexy Latinas in search of their Happily Ever Afters. She lives in Southern California with her husband, three kids, two Beagles, and one Bulldog, and is part of a larger, extended Mexican family whose members are NOT the source of inspiration for her characters. Or so she tells them.

Discover the **Delicious Desires** *series...*

DELICIOUS TEMPTATION

DELICIOUS SATISFACTION

If you love sexy romance, one-click these steamy Brazen releases...

FAKE ENGAGEMENT, REAL TEMPTATION
a *Passion and Protection* novel by Joya Ryan

Carrie Morgan goes on her Hawaiian honeymoon fantasy vacation to prove she's over her cheating ex—but he's there with his mistress in tow. How's she going to prove she's over him? Easy. One... Two... Three... She grabs her over-protective friend Blake and kisses him. Blake Harris knows better to give in to his best friend's sister...except he sees that broken look in Carrie's eyes. No. Hell no. New plan. He'll show her ex just what he's thrown away. The kisses? For show. The heat? Part of the performance. The private practice sessions? Uh-oh. Those are starting to feel a bit too real...

FOOLPROOF LOVE
a *Foolproof Love* novel by Katee Robert

Bull rider Adam Meyer put Devil's Falls in his rearview mirror years ago and hasn't stopped running since. Now he's back— temporarily, if he has any say about it. Restless, he finds himself kissing the sexiest girl in town...and agreeing to be the fake boyfriend in her little revenge scheme. It's going to be a wild ride!

LANDING THE AIR MARSHAL
a *Snowpocalypse* novel by Jennifer Blackwood

It was meant to be a one-night stand. One wicked night with an irresistibly sexy passenger. That's all Air Marshal Gage Michaels can afford—his career comes before everything else. Too bad the snowpocalpyse of the century has different plans for him and Abby Winters. Before the night's over, they find themselves snowed in at the most luxurious hotel in the city. But when it comes time to go, leaving is tougher than either of them could have imagined. They're two people who have nothing in common, living on opposite coasts. There's no way they can ever be together. Right?

SEDUCING THE BOSS
a *Pulse* novel by Mari Carr

Kellan James is at Score when he spots Sara Connelly—ER nurse, do-gooder, charitable crusader, and frequent pain in his ass. When Kellan discovers Sara's been stood-up, something fierce and protective awakens inside of him. Typically, Kellan would enjoy teasing the jilted Sara, but something in her face sends him over to her table with a plan. She accepts, but it quickly becomes apparent that one night isn't enough. As the pull between them grows stronger, Kellan discovers it's a very dangerous thing to say never.

Follow Me Under
a Follow Me novel by Helen Hardt

Dating Boston's billionaire bachelor has opened up a new world for Skye Manning. So why does she feel like she's losing herself? Braden Black never meant to fall for Skye, and he still tries to resist a relationship he knows he's not wired for. But not only has Skye awoken something inside him—he's stirring something dark and forbidden inside his Cinderella. Something even he can't control...

Like a Boss
an Accidentally Viral novel by Anne Harper

As if it wasn't bad enough that her long-term boyfriend dumped her, Nell Bennett goes viral online for ranting in a restaurant about her perpetually single status. Thankfully a kind and attractive stranger offers to share his table with her...and their sizzling banter leads to a surprising kiss before they part ways. Now her tiny hometown of Arbor Bay is buzzing over their latest Internet celebrity, but Nell's no stranger to attention. Still, even she never expected to show up to work only to discover her brand-new boss is a very familiar face...

WET AND RECKLESS
a Private Pleasures novel by Samanthe Beck

Aspiring singer/songwriter Roxy Goodhart's latest mistake is a doozy, involving a lying ex-manager, a dire lack of cash, and a teensy bit of grand larceny. Landing in the long, strong, entirely too tempting arms of the law is no way to keep a low profile. Taking an apartment puts her under orderly West Donovan and in his path every day. Testing his impressive reserve is beyond reckless, but she'd love to test it…all…night…long.

PLAYING WITH TROUBLE
a Sydney Smoke/Credence Crossover novel by Amy Andrews

Australian rugby pro Cole Hauser is ready for some peace and anonymity. The plan is perfect—until he discovers he's roomies with single mom Jane Spencer and her kid. While she's rehabbing the house in hopes it will put her business on the map, he's knee-deep in kid activities—and unexpectedly loving it. The situation is temporary, so it should be easy to say goodbye. However, it doesn't take long for them to realize they've borrowed a whole lot of trouble…but trouble never felt this good.